"Penn!" I screamed. "The house is on fire!"

I slept fitfully, a thin sleep full of uneasiness. In my dream something was wrong. I was drowning, flailing to get to the air. Then suddenly I awoke with a start, smoke stinging my nostrils. I couldn't make out the outline of the dressing table—only a slight shimmer of its mirror shone in the gray darkness. The room was full of smoke!

"Penn!" I cried. I shook his shoulder, coughing.

When he didn't move at once, cold fear gripped me. "Penn!" I screamed. "The house is on fire!"

Don't miss the other books in this exciting series,

T H E
SECRET
Diaries

VOLUME III
ESCAPE

JANICE HARRELL

47444

SCHOLASTIC INC.
New York Toronto London Auckland Sydney

ISBN 0-590-47691-2

Copyright © 1994 by Daniel Weiss Associates, Inc., and Janice Harrell. All rights reserved. Published by Scholastic Inc.

Produced by Daniel Weiss Associates, Inc.
33 West 17th Street, New York, NY 10011

12 11 10 9 8 7 6 5 4 3 2 1   4 5 6 7 8/9

Printed in the U.S.A.   01

First Scholastic printing, July 1994

For my husband.

ESCAPE

One

⟨⟨⟨❦⟩⟩⟩

Dear Diary,

I just woke up trembling. Everything seems so unreal to me. I have to remind myself who I am. I am Joanna Rigsby. My hair is as fair and straight as corn silk, I like to read, I love Penn Parrish—and lately I've been scared to death.

Outside the gently moving curtains of the bedroom, the gray light of dawn is touching the leaves. Penn is sprawled beside me, his mouth open and his breathing heavy. His eyelashes are like faint shadows against his cheeks, and a wrinkled sheet is pinned under his arm. I remember when I first saw Penn. He was sitting on the railing of the open passageway of Eastman wing; it was my first day at Barton High School. Penn's friends were with him, but I hardly noticed them. My gaze was fixed on him alone. His ash-blond hair caught the light, and he wore a white shirt with the sleeves rolled up to the elbows and the collar open at the throat. He was like a flash of radiance, the most absolutely beautiful thing I had ever seen, and I felt a sudden rush, as if . . . as if I were a violin string that had been touched and set humming. I didn't know it yet, but I had already begun to be drawn into murder.

Now, as I sit in bed next to Penn, listening to his even breathing, cold terror lies in the pit of my stomach. Diary, if I didn't keep you in code, I'd be afraid to write any of this down. As I write, my fingers are unsteady and the letters of the code are crooked and wobbly.

Last night I slept as if I had been knocked out. My senses shut down, I think, because there was so much I didn't want to think about.

But now that I'm awake, I am rigid with fear. Casey's death wasn't suicide, and Laurie's death wasn't an accident. Stephen is a murderer.

Penn stirred, then suddenly jerked awake, blinking at me. "What's wrong?" he asked thickly. "Are you okay?"

Okay. The word rang ironically in my ears, but I put my diary down and nodded.

Penn sat up suddenly. "Bad dreams?"

"I guess." I lowered my voice almost to a whisper. "Penn, I don't see how we can go on pretending we don't know what happened."

He pulled me close. "We can do it because we have to," he said quietly. "People can do pretty much anything that they have to do."

"I can't! Stephen will take one look at me and see what I'm thinking!"

Penn pushed my hair out of my eyes. "Nobody can read someone else's mind. You ought to know that."

He was right. If I had been able to read Stephen's mind, I would have known that he was going to kill Casey.

"Besides," Penn said, "it's not as if we've got to look really normal. Not one of us is normal lately. Stephen's drinking like a fish, and Tessa—haven't you noticed? She's like a puppet. She's all jerky."

"You mean even if I act weird, Stephen's not going to notice?"

"Right." He squeezed my hand. "All we've got to do is go on as if everything's fine." He reached for his bathrobe.

A minute later I heard Penn turning on the faucets in the bathroom. I picked up my diary again.

> Laurie is dead. Casey is dead. I'm still numb with the shock of realizing what that means.
>
> Now there are four of us left:
>
> Tessa West. Her shiny cap of dark hair and straight little nose are lovely, but the first thing I always notice about her is her baggy clothes. She looks as if she raided her big sister's closet. She's a good cook and poker player. She would do absolutely anything for Stephen.
>
> Stephen Garner. He and Tessa could be bookends. He is dark haired, too, and has brown eyes. He helps me with my physics. He's a chain-smoker, and lately I've been associating the smoky smell that clings to his clothes with getting all my homework problems right. And the most important thing about Stephen—he's a murderer.
>
> Penn Parrish. With Penn my cool assessment breaks down. I'm so in love with him, I can't look at him objectively anymore. I can't tell for sure whether he is really all that good

looking, or even whether he's a nice guy.

And then there's me, Diary. When I first met Penn, my life seemed full to bursting with wonderful possibilities. One happy day blurred into another. Blended together, the confused wash of memories meant happiness. But now it's different. Now, if I'm not careful, I know I can end up as dead as Laurie and Casey.

I have to act as if Penn and I haven't figured out that Stephen is a murderer. If only I can put the murders out of my mind and think about how much we used to like each other.

It's possible. All I need to do is to think of the sweet brilliance of Stephen's smile and forget that he is a killer.

I stared at the words I had just written. How could I ever forget that Stephen was a killer? I was terrified of him.

Neither of us said much when Penn got back from the bathroom. His hair was wet and slicked back on his head. We padded barefoot into the kitchen. The cabin was gray and eerily silent. Glancing outside at the colorless landscape, I shivered and put on the kettle. Then I switched on the kitchen light, but it did little to lift the gloom. I was moving carefully, trying not to make any noise that could waken Stephen and Tessa. Penn took fruit and butter from the fridge without saying a word. He put them on the counter, then silently gathered me into his arms and held me tight. I felt myself taking comfort in his familiar smell and his warmth. Suddenly the kettle's whistle shrieked. I leapt to pull it off the burner and it subsided with a few whimpering whistles. With a shaking hand I poured hot water onto the tea bag in my cup.

"Good morning!" said Stephen. When I looked up, he was standing near the fireplace. He was in jeans and a shirt, but his face was flushed with sleep and his hair was uncombed. I heard glass crash as if it were happening a long way off and felt at once a searing pain. I hardly noticed that the teacup had slipped from my fingers and that the hot water had darkened my jeans.

"Are you okay?" Penn asked. "Did you get burned?"

"The water wasn't that hot," I lied. "I'd better go change." I had to pass by Stephen to get back to the bedroom. The skin between my shoulder blades tightened as I accidentally touched him.

The silvery mirror showed my frightened face. I pulled off my jeans and shirt, blotted my skin dry, and slipped on a loose calico dress and sandals. A catbird cried harshly outside the curtains of the windows. A flutter of gray wings, and then the leaves moved as the bird disappeared.

Somehow I managed to make myself go back to the kitchen. I knew I couldn't leave Penn to carry on with the charade of breakfast by himself. When I got back to the living room, Tessa was at the dining-room table buttering squares of toast. She smiled at me and I saw that Penn was right. She did move jerkily, like a puppet.

Penn walked over to the big plate-glass window that overlooked the river, folded his hands behind him, and stared out. The sun had risen above the trees, and a rim of brilliance outlined his dark figure.

"I don't see what can go wrong," said Tessa suddenly into the silence.

Stephen's cup rattled in its saucer. "Let's not talk about it now, Tess," he said.

"What's the good of not talking about it," Tessa asked, "if everybody's thinking about it? Let's look at it coldly and rationally, huh? What can go wrong?"

Penn turned around, but he was so strongly

backlit, his face looked dark. "Nothing can go wrong," he said quietly. "Casey's death was a suicide, and the trail in Laurie's death leads away from us."

"That's what I'm thinking." Tessa glanced around at us. "So why can't we go back to being normal? What's the matter with everybody?"

"Maybe we aren't sleeping too well. Is anybody else not sleeping?" Stephen asked. "It's like we broke some taboo." He was speaking very quickly. "Do you know what I mean?"

"I don't see why you say that," protested Tessa. "Casey's death was an accident. The only reason we feel guilty is because he was getting to us so much that we really wanted him to die."

I wondered if she believed that. Stephen had gone to the computer lab intending to kill Casey. Penn and I knew that. How could Tessa not know it, too?

"We need to do something really fun! Something that will help us snap out of the blues," Tessa said. "Let's think of something."

There was a moment of silence. Then Penn said dryly, "We'll try."

I was rigid with fear, and it was hard not to look at Stephen. I wondered when he would try to kill us. Frightening images wheeled through my mind. I saw myself falling downstairs at school. Or plummeting out the window of one of the upstairs classrooms. Maybe my car would blow up, wired with explosives. An unknown mugger might attack me in a dark parking lot, leaving me dead. Or else a swollen can of tuna could lie by my body after I died agonizingly of some mysterious poison that was mistaken for botulism. No "accidental" death was too weird for me to imagine. It was a good thing that Stephen couldn't read my mind.

I walked behind the breakfast bar. "Does anyone want more toast?" I asked.

Tessa shook her head. "None for me, thanks. Have I mentioned that I've volunteered to work in the office at school?"

"You?" Penn's spoon clinked as he stirred sugar into his tea. "I didn't know you liked that kind of thing."

Tessa shrugged. "I'm going to have time on my hands," she said. "I've got the A.P. exams next Friday and Saturday, and once those are out of the way, I thought I might feel sort of bored. Now that we've already got our college acceptances, it's hard to get all that excited about school." She glanced around the table. "Do you see what I mean, or does that sound crazy?"

"The challenge of the copying machine," drawled Stephen. "The thrill of putting out the daily bulletins. Sure, we see why you want to volunteer in the office, Tess."

"It'll be something different," insisted Tessa. "It may turn out that I like it."

After breakfast Penn and Tessa played cards, and I wrote in my diary. Putting down in my own words what had happened made me feel as if I had power over the crazy events that were spinning out of control. I sensed Stephen's gaze on me, and my neck grew stiff with self-consciousness. *Murderer*, I thought. The word seemed to swell large and fill my brain.

Sun shone in the big window overlooking the river and made a yellow trapezoid on the waxed floor. The sun had ruined Casey's record, I remembered. Casey had played it until it grated on us like the sound of a fingernail on the blackboard. "*Je ne regrette rien*"—"I regret nothing"—the singer on the record had warbled over and over. I remember we were hurrying to pack and leave before a rainstorm broke and no one noticed what had become of the record. When we came back to the cabin later, we found it had been left leaning against the sunny window. It was warped. An accident, of course.

Stephen had a way of arranging accidents.

Later, Casey's blackmailing got brazen. Having Penn pick up an occasional dinner check wasn't enough for him anymore. Now keeping him happy required dangerously large amounts of cash, and none of us had that kind of money. What would we have done if Stephen hadn't killed Casey?

Penn touched my shoulder, and I jumped. "Want to take a walk?" he asked. At once I shut my diary and struggled up from the couch. I was relieved that Tessa and Stephen didn't offer to come along.

Outside, the sun beat on our heads. We escaped from it into the dark woods and picked our way along the trail. Ferns sprang damply up at the foot of a rise of gray rock, and the tops of trees pressed close one against the other, shutting out the sky and giving the air a hothouse feel. "I'm glad Stephen and Tessa didn't want to come along," said Penn, pushing back branches to let me pass.

"Maybe they're as sick of us as we are of them."

"Wouldn't that be great? The old gang could drift apart, no hard feelings."

"And then we'd all live happily every after." I

darted a quick glance at him. "But it's not going to happen that way, is it?"

"Why not?" asked Penn. He climbed precariously up a jagged rock, holding his hands out on either side for balance. He was freckled with the bits of sunlight escaping through the trees, and for a moment in the green forest light he belonged to another world, like a creature in an aquarium. Suddenly he leapt down, landing with a noisy rattle on a pile of dry leaves.

"Look at it this way," he said. "We aren't going to threaten to turn him in to the cops the way Laurie did or blackmail him the way Casey did. If we watch our step and don't do anything to make him nervous, we may get along okay."

I hoped Penn was right. I had noticed it was easier to feel optimistic in broad daylight than it was in the cold dim hours of the morning.

When we got back from our walk, Stephen and Tessa were in the living room playing cards. I sat down at the dining-room table to study my physics. Penn hurled himself into a chintz chair and pretended to do a crossword puzzle.

The minutes ticked by with unbearable slowness. I quit bothering to turn to the pages and stared blankly at my open physics book. At last Penn suggested that we might like to get back to town early. We all jumped at the idea and packed with indecent haste. The preparations to close up the cabin went by in a blur.

As Penn and I were driving home, the pines on either side of the road seemed to close in on us. I couldn't let my nerves get to me, I told myself, squirming a little. I had to be calm. I forced myself to fold my hands and let the faintly humming air-conditioning raise goose bumps on my arms.

"I think we did okay, don't you?" Penn asked.

"You mean it didn't show that I was falling apart?"

"Nah. Except for when the cup slipped out of your hand, you were fine." He hesitated. "I wonder what Tessa really thinks."

"What does it matter?" I cried. "You know she's on Stephen's side."

I used to find Tessa's loyalty one of her most attractive qualities. Now it was her loyalty to Stephen that made her so dangerous to us. Life is full of irony.

Penn's car swallowed up the road, racing over the pavement as it had so many times before, but the road was not the way I remembered, somehow. It seemed narrower.

"Do you think Tessa'd help Stephen kill us?" Penn asked.

"No," I said. "But I think she'd stand around afterward, saying it was too bad about our terrible accident."

The Corvette sped through the pine woods, cutting ruthlessly across the barred shadows that the trees threw across the road.

"Maybe we've got it wrong?" asked Penn suddenly. "Do we really think Stephen murdered them both?"

"It's easier to believe at two A.M., when you're hearing funny noises outside," I pointed out. "I've noticed that. Sure, it seems kind of strange thinking about it now, but that doesn't mean the murders didn't happen. They did."

Penn shot me a quick glance. "Do you think he could be crazy? I mean, actually out of his mind?"

I shook my head.

"Even when you see what happened with your own eyes," he said, "it's unreal."

"Is this where I'm supposed to say it's all a bad dream?"

"No." He shook his head. "I know I'm not making any sense."

Penn's hair feathered softly where it touched the nape of his neck. I loved everything about him, his clear skin and his soft, dark lashes.

Tenderness toward him overcame me. I can't die now, I thought. It would be too cruel.

"There's one good thing," said Penn. "Next weekend Stephen and Tessa are both going to be in those A.P. tests. At least they won't expect to come out to the cabin with us."

I exhaled. Two days, at least, that I didn't have to worry about.

Two

"Penn, my diary is missing!"

Penn's voice on the other end of the telephone line was reassuring. "Are you sure you've looked everywhere?"

"Where am I supposed to look?" I cried desperately. "I dumped out my duffel bag and it wasn't there."

The hands of the clock on the kitchen wall jerked to four o'clock.

"When did you see it last?" he asked.

"At the cabin this morning. I remember I was writing in it before breakfast. About Stephen." I gulped. "About the murders."

The silence was strained. At last Penn said, "Are you positive you don't have it? Maybe you unpacked it and forgot."

17

"How could I do that?" I asked. "I only un-packed fifteen minutes ago. Look—the bag wasn't completely zipped up. Maybe it fell out in the trunk. Would you check?"

"Sure. I'll go out and look and get back to you."

I sat by the phone, gnawing on my knuckles, but Penn didn't call me back, and when I dialed his number, I got no answer. I gazed forlornly out the big window in the dining room. I should have been worried, I suppose, about Stephen's getting hold of my diary, but I wasn't thinking about that. Instead, I ached at its loss. How could I get on without it? I thought unhappily. It had been my link to sanity in the days when I begged my father to let me come and live with him, and then struggled to make a new life for myself in yet another strange school. I had writ-ten in my diary about the first time Penn had kissed me and when he had sent me red roses on Valentine's Day. I had poured all my hopes and my nightmares onto its pages.

On the golf course beyond the lake behind our house, a tournament seemed to be going on. A clump of people were following the golfers around, and I could make out a grandstand that had been erected to the east, near the road. The scene looked insanely placid, and I wanted to scream at them or throw a firecracker—anything to shatter their calm.

Minutes later I heard Penn's car driving up. I dashed out the front door and down the steps, but I saw at once by his expression that he hadn't found my diary. He climbed out of the car. "I thought I'd come help you look," he said.

"It's not here!" I cried. "Don't you think I've looked?"

"Then I guess we drive out to the cabin and check there."

I climbed into Penn's car, trying to convince myself that my diary was at the cabin. I remembered stuffing it in my duffel bag before we left, but maybe I was mistaken.

As the car's engine hummed, I hugged myself, and my fingers kneaded the flesh of my forearm. We passed a billboard that said in large letters FRIENDS DON'T LET FRIENDS DRIVE DRUNK.

Friends. The word echoed bitterly in my mind. We had been such close friends and so happy. How could it be that now we were sick with fear and eyeing each other with mistrust?

We bumped down the dirt driveway, and the cabin loomed before us, its big plate-glass window flashing silver in the light.

Penn turned the key in the front door and we stepped inside. A quick glance around showed no sign of the diary, and my heart sank. Then the thorough search began. We looked under the chairs and the couch. We tossed sofa and chair cushions off and probed with our fingers in the creases of the slipcovers. In our bedroom Penn tugged off the bed linens and checked under the pillows and bed. The other beds got the same treatment. We opened kitchen cabinets and even looked in the refrigerator.

Penn's eyes had a look of painful concentration. "It's not here," he said at last.

"Stephen must have taken it," I said. "All he needed was a minute alone with my duffel bag while we were carrying things to the car. He's seen me stuff my diary in on top of my clothes lots of times. He'd know right where to look for it. I feel so stupid! Leaving my bag unwatched like that! Dumb!" I slapped my forehead.

Penn stood up. "There's nothing we can do about it now," he said. "Let's go back to town and get something to eat."

We were both silent on the drive back to town. Penn actually slowed down to thirty-five when the speed limit changed at the city limits, which showed how shaken he was. WELCOME TO

BARTON CITY, said the sign. It was covered with tarnished medallions the size of plates. Kiwanis Club, Elks Club, Rotary Club welcomed us. Over the signs spilled a spray of wild roses, their pink matching the faded red of a crushed fried-chicken carton that lay on the grass.

"Maybe for now," Penn suggested hesitantly, "you could drive to school a different way. Maybe you should change the route you take when you go to classes, too. You know?"

"Next we get matching bulletproof vests," I said.

"Seriously, we don't know what he might try," said Penn.

"Maybe we're panicking for no reason."

"Maybe. But we can't count on it. Remember how he kept harping on whether Casey was going to turn state's evidence? He's got to be thinking the same thing about us."

Especially if he reads my diary, I thought miserably.

"I remember he sat up all night trying to think of some exotic poison that would kill Casey without leaving a trace," said Penn bitterly. "For all I know he's getting ready to sprinkle arsenic on our meat loaf."

"He's not going to do that. He'll think up something new, not something he talked to you about."

"I'm not sure of anything. What I keep think-ing is that it must be a lot easier to kill when you're doing it for the third time."

This gloomy observation put a damper on any further conversation. It seemed crazy to be going on with our lives as if nothing had happened, when we might be being pursued by a murderer.

We ate at a small Chinese restaurant. Inside were Formica tables and faded travel posters of China. An ornate red lacquer lamp hung over a gum machine next to the take-out counter. The food was ordinary. I knew that the reason we had come was that Stephen would never think to look for us here.

Even so, I found myself often glancing up from my moo goo gai pan to check the door. Every time the tinny little bell tinkled over the door, I jumped.

Penn glanced over his shoulder, saw that the customer was a fat, middle-aged woman, and re-turned to his egg roll. "So what exactly is in this diary of yours?" he asked.

"Everything!"

Penn's fork traced a pattern on his plate. "You mean you've put in everything we've been talk-ing about—about Laurie's and Casey's murders?" He glanced up at me quickly.

I nodded.

"I thought you were always behind when it came to writing in your diary." Penn sliced his egg roll savagely. "How come all of a sudden you're caught up?"

I licked my lips. "Writing in it calms me down. When I woke up early yesterday, I sat up in the bed and wrote for quite a while. But it was in code, Penn. That's why I wasn't worried about it. Every word I've written in it has been in code."

"I hope it's a good code," he said.

At school the next morning, I came upon Stephen and Tessa making out in the shadows of a stairwell. I wasn't sure whether I should speak to them or not. But before I could decide, Stephen turned around to face me. "Hold up, Joanna." His tone was offhand. "I've got something for you." He rummaged in his book bag, then made a pitching gesture. My diary spun in the air and landed in my outstretched hands.

"I don't know how it ended up in my bag," he said. "I guess I was packing in too much of a hurry yesterday."

"Thanks," I whispered.

Without looking back, I fled.

Dear Diary,

It feels so strange to be writing in you now! I keep leafing through your pages over and over, feeling shivery. Has Stephen been reading my secrets? Even the paper seems different now. But I know Stephen can't have ruined my diary. It's impossible. It still gives me the creeps to know he's rifled through these pages. The letters of the code swim in my vision and are like indistinct gray lines that mean nothing.

Three

"He pitched you the diary in the hall," said Penn when we met outside the cafeteria. "Just like that? No explanation?"

"He said he must have put it in his bag accidentally because he was in a hurry."

Penn's gray eyes were troubled. "I wonder if there's any chance he's telling the truth."

"No! He's lying! Do you really believe he thought my diary was a piece of his underwear? Stephen never brings books to the cabin, Penn. It's not as if he could have gotten my diary mixed up with something of his. He took it on purpose."

Penn put his hand on my shoulder and turned me around. "I can't face going in there and eating lunch with them today," he said. "I can't."

I felt the same way. It was a relief not to have to

25

go into the cafeteria. Penn and I got peanut-butter crackers and soft drinks from the vending machine and sat together at the foot of the back stairs of Haggerty wing. From there we could see the Dumpster where Casey had parked his old Chevy the night he died. When I first moved to Barton City, the town had seemed bland. In those days a fire hydrant was a fire hydrant to me and a Dumpster was a Dumpster. Now everything my eyes lit on buzzed with meaning. The Dumpster wasn't an inert collection of metal and trash. Now it marked the last place Casey had parked. It seemed to gaze back at me pointedly, like a finger of blame.

"Let me see the diary," said Penn.

I pushed it over to him.

"Any signs that Stephen's been reading it?" he asked. "Any drops of chocolate milk or finger marks on it?"

"The paper seems different somehow," I said.

Penn laughed suddenly, his eyes crinkling into amused triangles. "Your nerves are getting to you. He can't have soaked the pages in poison without making the ink run."

"I know." I shrugged. "It's only a feeling I have. I guess it's like when a burglar gets into your house. The place feels funny afterward, even if nothing was taken."

Penn weighted the right-hand page down with his package of crackers to keep it open, and reached for his pencil. "Let's have a go at the code," he said.

He frowned a moment at the pages, then pointed to some single letters—*l* and *x*. "Okay," he said, "one of those has to be *I* and one has to be *A*, because those are pretty much the only single-letter words."

He wrote "*l* = A/I" and "*x* = A/I."

I tensed up. Already I could see where this was leading.

He chewed on his pencil, narrowing his eyes in concentration. "All right, several times on one page we find a four-letter word where the last two letters are identical. My guess is that this one is likely to be 'Penn.'" He glanced up at me. "Double final letters aren't all that common in ordinary words. It pretty much has to be a name, and what name is more likely to show up again and again in your diary than mine?"

He wrote out "LYKK," and under it the letters "PENN." "Okay," he continued, "the other word we'll look for is 'the,' since it's got to keep showing up again and again, almost every time we have a noun. We already know that the last letter of 'the' is going to be *y*, because we found that out when we learned how to spell 'Penn' in the code. Ah! Here it is, I'll bet. P, ƒ, y must spell 'the.' So now we've got the code-letter equivalents for five or six letters. Let's write them down in order and see if we've got a pattern yet."

He made two lines of letters on the paper, one for the regular alphabet and one for the code. Like this:

A — xz		N — k
B —		O —
C —		P — l
D —		Q —
E — y		R —
F —		S —
G —		T — p
H — f		U —
I — xz		V —
J —		W —
K —		X —
L —		Y —
M —		Z —

He studied his chart a moment. "Looks like they're sort of in order, but not quite." He narrowed his eyes. "Something funny's going on with the vowels. They don't seem to fit in the regular order. Okay, let's go after the vowels. We'll take

every two- or three-letter word and pick out a
letter that has to be a vowel. There are only five
vowels, so we can narrow these down pretty fast."

"Stop," I said, putting my hand over his chart.
"I can see how easy it's going to be to break it.
You don't have to go on."

Penn shook a strand of hair out of his eyes.
"No, you'd better let me go on. Let me see how
long it takes."

It took him fifteen minutes. I had, after all,
made up the code when I was only in the fifth or
sixth grade, and it was pretty simple. Completely
exposed, it looked like this:

A — x		N —k
B — a		O —.
C — b		P —l
D — c		Q —m
E — y		R —n
F — d		S —o
G — e		T —p
H — f		U —q
I — z		V —r
J — g		W—s
K — h		X —t
L — i		Y —u
M— j		Z —

"I figured I wouldn't use z much," I said lamely.

Penn grinned. "That was when you didn't realize what a zoo it was around here." But his smile faded quickly. "So what you did was substitute the less-used letters like x, y, and z for the vowels, and then you bumped all the other letters over one, except for o."

"Yeah. I plugged in a dot for the o. Easy to remember. In fact, I've been able to write the entire code without thinking for years," I said. "Like this." I took the pen from him and wrote "Z I.RY U.Q."

He smiled. "I love you, too. But this is bad, Joanna. One thing we know now for sure. It wouldn't have taken him long to work out the code. Stephen's bound to have read whatever is in this diary."

"Ouch!"

Penn closed the diary. "We're going to have to be really careful from now on. I'm not kidding. I don't want you to take any chances. He knows that we know he's a murderer, and he may panic."

I looked at him in dismay. "What are we going to do?"

"I'm not sure. I've got to think. I'm going to

call my mother in Maryland and see if she'll let us come stay with her."

"But what about school?" I cried. "What about graduation?"

"We'll take the GED if we have to," said Penn impatiently. "A diploma's not going to be much good to us if we're lying in the morgue."

"Even if Stephen did read the diary, Penn, all he knows is that we think he's a murderer. I never said anything at all about going to the police."

"He was worried enough to steal it, wasn't he?" asked Penn. "And he didn't even try to hide what he'd done, either. That's not a good sign."

A hot tear spilled onto my cheek. "I wish I'd never kept a diary!" I cried.

Penn squeezed my shoulder. "Hey, I'm the one who got you into this. Don't go beating up on yourself. It might not have made any difference. Stephen could have gone after us next, whether you'd kept a diary or not. At least this way we know to be on our guard."

I knew he was only trying to make me feel better.

When I got home from school, the evening paper was lying rolled up in the driveway. I glanced guiltily across the street as I bent to pick it up. Bobby Jenkins's car was parked in his driveway, so he had to be at home. Lately I had been trying to avoid him. Even catching a glimpse of him at a distance upset me. I was afraid it showed on my face that I had helped hide the truth about Laurie's death. He was Laurie's stepbrother, but they had been more to each other than that. The ring he had given her had been found on her body. *Love, forever. B.* was engraved inside the band.

Guilt gnawed at me whenever I saw him. And fear. He had vowed to kill her murderer if he could get his hands on him, and from what I knew of Bobby, he did not seem the sort to make fine distinctions between accomplices and the actual killer.

I went inside, spread the newspaper out on the kitchen table, and began scanning it. Red Cross Blood Drive Exceeds Goal. Highway Crash Claims Five. I had been reading the paper very closely the past few months. It gave me my only clues about the progress the police were making. Leafing over to the inside section, I was startled to see a grainy photograph of Stephen captioned in bold black letters with his last name, GARNER. The story read:

LOCAL TEEN NAMED NATIONAL MERIT SCHOLAR

> *Evanston, Il.* As one of 2,000 high
> school seniors chosen from across the
> United States, Barton City's Stephen
> Garner was named a National Merit
> Scholar. The honor carries with it a
> $2000 scholarship.
>
> Garner, who ranks second in his
> class at Barton City High, is the son
> of James and Alix Garner of Melody
> Lane.

No mention of his being a murderer. But
then, that wasn't the sort of extracurricular ac-
tivity Stephen would have listed. He had wanted
the National Merit Scholarship bad, and I was
surprised he hadn't mentioned that he had gotten it. He must have known. But when I thought
back over the past few weeks, I realized he had
far more important things on his mind. Like getting rid of Casey. Casey had put all this at risk,
the tidy little scholarship, the long-expected
honor. Only Penn and I were a risk to him now. I
folded the paper neatly and put it away. I went
over to the sink and ran some water into a tumbler full of ice. Suddenly my mouth was dry.

At school the next day I had the sensation I was in a fun house, surrounded by those wavy mirrors that make everyone look accordion pleated and fat and thin in all the wrong places. Smiles were grotesque. Any sudden gestures looked threatening. I couldn't control my growing sense of panic.

"Joanna!"

I wheeled around, startled, but it was only Nikki Warren. She came over to me, showing an astonishing number of white teeth in a broad grin. When she drew close I could see the gums above her teeth. "I wanted to let you know that your suggestion that the senior class gift should be picnic tables outside the cafeteria is going on the ballot," she said. "The committee thought it was a really good suggestion."

"Oh," I said. "Good."

Nikki lowered her voice, and her face suddenly became a parody of sober concern. "What we're thinking about now is some kind of meaningful memorial to the seniors who won't graduate with us."

I was so completely freaked out that at first I didn't get her drift. "Won't they go to summer school and graduate later?" I asked.

"I mean Laurie and Casey," she said.

"Oh."

"Some people thought a good memorial would be a tasteful plaque in the office, with their pictures, you know? But other people said maybe we should plant some flowers."

Nikki had the energy and optimism of a Disney cartoon character. Her neatly pressed clothes, the tiny gold studs in her ears, her hoarse, froggy voice, and her unquenchable wholesomeness grated unbearably. As if I were looking through a telescope into the future, I could see Nikki in stout shoes addressing the garden club, Nikki peering over spectacles to address the PTA meeting, Nikki keeping the kids in line while she drove the car pool, her froggy voice repeating relentlessly in the years to come, "Remember, if you're not part of the solution, you're part of the problem."

I pressed my fingers to my temples and squeezed my eyes closed.

"Do you need an aspirin?" Nikki asked. "I always carry aspirin, Band-Aids, and a safety pin. You never can tell when something like that's going to come in handy."

"No." I shook my head. "No, really, I'm fine."

"Oh. Okay, if you say so. What do you think, then? Plaque or flowers?"

"Flowers," I said. The last thing I wanted was to have to face a picture of Casey smirking at me every time I went by the office.

She jotted my vote down on her notebook and flashed me a smile. I watched as her small, neat figure bobbed out of sight down the crowded hall, feeling a twinge that at first I couldn't identify. Then, suddenly and unexpectedly, it came to me—I envied her.

I had met Nikki my first day at school. She had shown me the way to my physics class and had warned me against getting involved with Penn and his bunch. What was it she had said? "That's a very tight clique." Was it she who had said that, or someone else? I wasn't sure anymore. But I remember clearly that she had said, "Those guys aren't what you'd think just by looking at them." She had been more right about that than she knew, but on that first day I had been secretly amused and had thought only that she wasn't cool. She cared about school spirit, for instance, and nobody cared about school spirit anymore. I seem to remember that I felt slightly superior to her.

When Penn had picked me up and swooped away with me in his beautiful red car, I had been drunk with victory—it was like being the star of a movie. I had loved being part of his bunch, sharing in their jokes and their secrets, included on the weekends at the cabin. But today I would happily trade places with Nikki Warren. Except for Penn, I thought. I would not be willing to give up Penn.

At lunchtime Penn and I went into the cafeteria together, bracing ourselves to face Stephen. But it turned out that Stephen and Tessa weren't there. We kept an eye out for them, but they never showed up.

"We've got to eat," I said. I was suddenly struck by how unappetizing the food looked.

"Funny, isn't it?" Penn smiled wistfully. "Yesterday they were here and we didn't show up. Today we're here and they don't show up."

Four

Dear Diary,

Is it stupid to keep writing in the code
when I know Stephen must have broken it?
Should I stop keeping a diary? I don't know.
Who else can I tell my secrets to? I'm scared
and I can't let anybody know. A history
teacher explained to me once that armies
make soldiers shine their shoes and keep
themselves clean and neat because it's a way
of maintaining morale. Morale—I guess
that's another word for not going crazy with
fear. Writing in my diary is like that. It's a
tiny bit of order in my life that keeps me sane.

Later that afternoon I was driving back from
the drugstore with a plastic bag on the seat beside

me. I had bought shampoo, sun block, and a small pack of antihistamine as if I planned to live through a normal sneezing, sunburnt summer. But I couldn't forget, when I looked at the bag, that my summer could be snuffed out in an instant. Stephen could see to that. I checked the rearview mirror, watching for any sign of his motorcycle.

I had been driving only a few minutes when it dawned on me that the car ahead of me was Bobby's. It was weaving erratically. I glanced around wildly, hoping a cop would materialize out of nowhere and stop his car, but all I saw was a pizza delivery truck and a station wagon full of kids. Both vehicles changed lanes and sped ahead, giving Bobby's car a wide berth. As we approached City Lake, Bobby's car stopped at the red light. I took a deep breath and argued with my conscience. Suddenly, without giving myself time to think about it any longer, I opened my door, jumped out, and ran up to his car.

"Bobby?" I was staggered to see that he had buried his face in his arms on the steering wheel. His back was heaving with sobs. I reached in the open window and touched his shoulder. "Bobby, are you all right?"

"Leave me alone," he muttered. A loud sniffle, and then he wiped his forearm over his nose. His face was red.

The light changed and the car behind mine honked. "Do you need to talk?" I asked him. "Why don't we go somewhere and grab something to eat." The guy behind my car was leaning on his horn. I glanced back at him nervously. Then, as he continued to honk, I ran back to my car.

"Visit with the boyfriend on your own time, sister," the man screamed out the window.

My ears burned as I stepped on the gas. I wished I hadn't gotten out to check on Bobby. What did I care if he crashed his car? Besides, I told myself, it was a waste of time. He wasn't drunk after all, so I hadn't saved his life or anything. And he hadn't paid the slightest attention to my invitation to talk. I could have saved myself the trouble.

Then suddenly, to my surprise, Bobby made a U-turn, doubled back, and turned into the parking lot of a diner. Blinking with astonishment, I followed his lead. I had no choice now. After avoiding him for weeks, I had to sit down with him face-to-face. My pulse fluttered in panic. What was I going to say to him?

When I pushed the door open, I smelled fresh

coffee and newly baked bread. Bobby was sitting in a booth, frowning at a bagel.

I got a cup of hot tea and took it over to him. His sheer bulk seemed to overwhelm the small booth. "Hi," I said. I sat down across from him. A few zits and some patches of stubble gave his face an ill-kept appearance. He looked like a career criminal fresh out on parole.

"Hi," he said.

"Are you okay?" I asked. "Your car was swerving all over the place."

"I guess I'd better pull myself together before I get back in the car," he said.

"Rough day?" I ventured.

"I went out to Laurie's grave."

I sucked in my breath.

"The grass has grown over it," he said. "You wouldn't expect that this soon, would you?"

"Maybe they sod it or something."

"Maybe. I swear, for a minute there I felt like digging up the grass with my bare hands and getting in there with her. It was so empty out there, you know? No people, no animals. Just flowers. Laurie always liked to have people around. It gives me the creeps to think she's out there all by herself."

I could feel the hairs on the back of my neck

rising. He was speaking of Laurie in the present tense.

"I guess you think I'm nuts, don't you?" he growled.

"No!" I protested, a bit too fast. "Not at all."

"Sometimes I think I am going nuts," he said slowly. "I never even thought about it before, but murder is a terrible thing." He leaned over the table and regarded me with bloodshot eyes.

I gulped. "I know," I said. "It's tough."

He banged his open hand on the table. The lady at the counter jumped and looked over at us in alarm.

"They say you start to feel better bit by bit," I suggested, "but it takes time."

He laughed bitterly. "Didn't take Penn and them long to get over it, did it?"

"Everybody grieves a little differently, I guess," I said uncomfortably.

"Don't go telling me that bunch did any crying for Laurie," he snorted. "Bunch of . . . I never did like them. I tried to tell Laurie they didn't care about her." He stared down at his bagel, slightly puzzled. "I never did get what she saw in them, but they'd all been hanging around together since the year one, so I had to watch what I said. I had to be subtle about it."

I smiled to myself at the idea of Bobby being subtle.

He glanced up at me. "There's something fishy about that whole setup. I can't figure it out exactly, but something's not right. Laurie always said they didn't take drugs, but I wonder if she knew everything that went on."

"They're okay," I said uncomfortably. I knew they weren't okay at all. "And really they don't take drugs. It's just that you and they are on different wavelengths, that's all."

"I hate those jerks!" he cried. "When I see them walking around acting like everything's just great when they know Laurie's been murdered—murdered!—I just want to strangle them." He was breathing heavily, and I found myself staring in fascination at his huge hands, the fingers working. "They've got no hearts, you know what I mean? I never could figure out what a nice girl like Laurie was doing hooked up with them." His watery eyes gazed at me in puzzlement.

I made a helpless gesture.

"Ever since Casey killed himself," Bobby's eyes narrowed, "I keep thinking something's going on. Don't you think? Why would he kill himself? I never saw anybody more full of himself than Casey was. Why, he's the last person—"

Bobby shook his shaggy head slowly. "I don't know. I can't figure it out." He slapped his hand on the table rhythmically. "I just wish I'd quit hurting."

I reached out to pat him, but he pulled away.

"I've got to get it together," he said. "It's not going to do Laurie or anybody any good if I wreck my car."

Suddenly I had a horrible impulse to tell Bobby the truth. Stephen murdered Laurie, I wanted to shout. The relief would be incredible. I wouldn't be shielding Stephen anymore. Bobby would kill him for us, or at the very least permanently disable him, and we would be safe. I closed my eyes and gripped the edge of the table with my thumbs.

"Are you all right?" asked Bobby. "I haven't been getting you down talking about this, have I?"

"No." I licked my lips. "I'm so sorry about Laurie." Suddenly I knew I couldn't tell Bobby the truth. Not so much for Stephen's sake as for Bobby's. I couldn't make him into a murderer.

"You're a nice girl, Jo," he said. The booth shuddered as Bobby shoehorned himself out of it. He smiled down at me. "I just don't like the bunch you run around with."

I watched the door swing closed behind him.

"Want a refill on that tea?" called the woman at the counter.

I shook my head and gulped the tea down.

A sudden draft made me look up at the opening door. I stiffened. It was Stephen. "Hi," he said lazily. He ambled over to me and rested his splayed fingertips on the table so close that his nicotine-stained finger almost touched my saucer. "What could you have been talking to Bobby about?" he asked. His voice was silky.

I stared up at him in stupefied silence for a moment. "He was out visiting Laurie's grave, and he was upset," I said. "I didn't say much, actually. I mostly listened."

Stephen passed a hand over his mouth. "Jeez, I didn't know what to think when I saw the two of you doing U-turns in the middle of the road. Then I saw you were coming in here together." His eyes were darker than bitter chocolate.

"What did you think we were doing?" I asked him. "Plotting against you?" As soon as the words were out of my mouth, I regretted them, but Stephen only laughed unsteadily, and for an instant he seemed like the old Stephen, the one I had trusted.

He shook his head slowly. "I don't know," he said. "It was so weird, that's all. You two are coming in here together and I'm thinking, well, heck, you hardly know him. What do you want to talk to him for?"

"We're neighbors. Bobby lives across the street."

"But it's not like you really know him, is it?" he asked. I realized Stephen was asking me for reassurance. Incredible though it might be, he seemed to want me to promise him that Bobby and I weren't plotting against him.

"I saw his car weaving," I said. "That's all. I thought maybe he was drunk, and I got out of my car to check on him. But it turned out he wasn't drunk, he was upset, so I said maybe he'd like to talk. That's all there was to it."

"Simple human kindness, huh?"

"Something like that."

He sat down across from me and leaned across the table. "So, what'd Bobby have to say?" he asked. His black irises were large, highlighted with a tiny gleam of reflected light. "I'd really like to know," he added softly.

Uneasily I remembered that Bobby had mostly talked about how Casey's death looked fishy. I couldn't tell Stephen that. "Nothing much," I said finally. "He talked about Laurie. And how sad he was."

"He didn't mention me—or Penn?"

"Well, he doesn't like either of you. You know that."

Stephen's mouth twisted. "So he did mention us, huh?"

I felt backed into a corner. "Only in a general sort of way. He said he never did understand why Laurie liked you." My heart was racing. Avoiding his eyes, I looked out the glass front of the diner. Some kids were carrying a basket to the pet shop next door. Three old ladies, one of them with a cane, were slowly getting into a station wagon outside. Normal, quiet scenes. Innocent people running innocent errands. I wished I were one of them.

"So you told him what fine people we were, I guess." Stephen's voice startled me.

Suddenly I looked him straight in the eye. "What is this all of a sudden, Stephen? The third degree?"

He ran his fingers through his hair. "Okay, I guess I'm making a fool of myself." He took a deep breath. "I don't know why. You know that we've all been kind of on edge lately, since . . ." His voice trailed off.

"Since poor Casey killed himself," I finished for him.

I glanced over my shoulder at the lady in the

pink apron who was wiping off the counter. She could probably hear every word we were saying. I was going to have to be careful.

"Yeah," said Stephen in a choked voice. "Like you say."

I cleared my throat, eager to change the subject. "I haven't had a chance to congratulate you about getting the National Merit Scholarship."

"What?" He looked blank.

"The National Merit Scholarship," I repeated. "It was in the paper. That's quite an honor, isn't it?"

He shrugged. "I guess. I haven't thought about it much. I've had kind of a lot on my mind lately, you know?"

Like murdering Casey, I thought. I had to stop thinking of how Stephen had killed Casey or I was going to say something stupid. I gulped. "Do you want a bagel or anything?"

Stephen shook his head. "I don't think so," he said. He pressed the bowl of my spoon so the handle popped up and then let it clatter noisily to the table. I felt unbearably self-conscious. Stephen's banging the silverware about was sure to draw attention to us. I ached to get up and run away.

"Lots of people think I'm ambitious, you

know," Stephen said suddenly, glancing up at me. "But it's not me who's ambitious—it's Tessa. She's the one who wanted to get into Princeton. All I want is to be with her."

"You'll get to see plenty of her," I said. "Rutgers isn't that far away, is it?"

"Too far." He shrugged. "Well, I tried and it didn't work out."

"It doesn't matter. You'll still get to see her lots."

"It matters. But there's nothing I can do about it." To my relief he stood up. "Well, I guess I'd better go study for the stupid A.P. exams." He smiled unsteadily. "Since I've already paid for them and everything."

"Good luck."

"I don't believe in luck." He met my eyes. "I guess you and Penn are going to the cabin this weekend."

I jumped. The last thing I wanted was for Stephen to know where we were going. "Oh, I don't know."

He smiled. "Sure, you'll go out there. I know Penn pretty well, you know. He probably can't wait to have the cabin to himself, just you and him there together. Heck, it's his favorite place."

"Actually," I said, "we're talking about going to the beach, instead."

"Sounds like fun. Well, when you're playing volleyball in the surf, think of poor Tessa and me slaving away on the A.P. exams."

After he left, I sat alone in the booth until I became aware that the lady at the counter was staring at me curiously. I hastily scrambled to my feet.

I knew Penn was at the library. My one thought was that I had to get to him. I drove directly there.

I found Penn at a dusty table in the back room, next to the genealogy shelves. He was slouched down so low in his chair that its back pressed against the base of his neck. On his stomach was balanced a science-fiction novel.

"I thought you were working on your research paper," I said.

He shook his head. "One way or another, we aren't going to finish the year here, so what's the point?"

I sat down suddenly, my knees weak.

"What's wrong?" Penn sat up and closed his book. "You look like you've seen a ghost."

I shook my head. "No. Stephen." Checking around first to make sure no one was close enough to hear what we were saying, I told him what had happened.

"Too bad we can't tell Bobby the truth." Penn

folded the book closed and put it on the table. "I bet he'd take care of Stephen for us."

"No, Penn. Don't even say it."

"I was just joking. Even if I felt like doing it, and believe me, I don't, who's to say Bobby wouldn't go in for a wholesale massacre of everybody who was mixed up in it? There's something uncivilized about old Bobby."

It struck me that Penn's assessment of Bobby was all wrong. Maybe Bobby was in some ways more civilized than the rest of us. After all, didn't it make more sense to cry about Laurie's death than to get mixed up in a crazy scheme to cover it up, the way Penn had? "Bobby's okay," I said.

"I wish you'd quit saying that," Penn said irritably.

I sat down next to him and reached for his hand. The next thing I knew he had pulled me into his lap and was planting a kiss on my neck. As we clung to each other, a languorous spell fell over me. Time and space seemed suspended, and I touched the corner of his mouth with my finger, loving the curve of his lip and the long sensitive line of his mouth. Then I pressed my lips against his until I could feel his breath coming fast. He reached awkwardly around to embrace me and suddenly the science-fiction novel fell to the floor with a sound like a slap. We jerked as if we had been hit by an electric shock.

Someone cleared his throat. I looked around and saw the unkempt, short man who silently shelved books in the library. He was balding and stoop shouldered. He was pushing a book trolley full of books into a nearby aisle to be reshelved, and a second later he had silently disappeared between the stacks of books.

Suddenly self-conscious, I slid off Penn's lap.

Penn shot a glance at the aisle where the library assistant had disappeared. "He's like some sinister little gnome, isn't he?" he said.

"Cut it out, Penn. It's not his fault we're in a mess."

"Jeez, I know it. You're right. I take it all back." He pressed his palm to his forehead. "Look, did Stephen sound as if he was threatening you?" he asked. "I don't feel like I've got a clear picture. I mean, do you think he was following you and came into the diner on purpose to get you rattled?"

"I don't know. Bobby and I did U-turns right in the middle of Sunset Avenue. We were pretty conspicuous. It could have been an accident that he saw us."

"Accident," snorted Penn. "I've gotten to where I hate that word."

"He asked if we were going out to the cabin this weekend. I told him we weren't. I said we were going to the beach."

"Good." Penn looked relieved. "I'm glad you told him that. Now we don't have to worry. At least not this weekend."

Footsteps grated on the gritty vinyl floor. The library assistant pushed the trolley out into our line of sight once more.

"How do I know he believed me?" I said. "I don't know if we should go to the cabin. Maybe you and I ought to do something completely different. Something he'd never suspect. We could go to Raleigh and stay in a motel."

"You're kidding, right?"

I could almost feel the pull of the cabin on Penn. Stephen was right—it was his favorite place in the world. And we would never have a safer time to go there than this weekend, when Stephen was preoccupied with the A.P. tests and thought we were at the beach.

"Oh, okay," I said suddenly. "Let's go to the cabin. Why not?"

Penn smiled. His eyes were half-closed as he pulled me back onto his lap.

"Penn!" I protested. "People can see us."

"Who cares?" he whispered in my ear.

While we kissed, the squeak of the wheels of the book trolley grew fainter. Penn was right, I thought. When we could die tomorrow, what could it possibly matter what the book gnome might think of us?

Five

. . . Funny how Penn's love can make me feel safe. It's crazy. When we're kissing, I forget that Stephen is probably stalking us. I even lose track of time. We might be clinging together, spinning like a planet in a gloriously safe universe. But when I pull away from him, a chill settles over my heart. Maybe this is our last kiss, I think. Maybe Stephen is waiting for us now, outside.

It had rained Friday night, and when we got to the cabin at midday on Saturday, puddles lay in the dirt driveway, their surfaces coated with a thin yellow film of tree pollen. Some fuzzy caterpillars had floated down onto the front stoop. We brushed them away when we brought our bags up the steps. A handful of white blossom petals clung to the weather-roughened wood of the railing. Penn unlocked the door and I followed him in, tossing my duffel bag to the floor.

Penn looked around. "Don't you love it here? I feel great the minute I step in the door." He smiled and swept me into his arms. We stood there for several minutes, nuzzling each other and laughing softly.

"Hey, let's get something to eat," Penn said.

He strode over to the kitchen and flung open the fridge. "What'll it be?" He grinned. "Bread-and-butter sandwiches? Or do we bring in the groceries from the car?"

I felt a surge of relief that the cabin had worked its spell yet again. It didn't matter that Tessa wasn't here with us to bake cookies and omelets. It didn't matter that outside a cloud of danger and death threatened to swallow us up. Sunlight gleamed on the river as it ran past the overhanging trees in their new greenery, and the blossoms of spring were showering down on the earth. Penn flung open the kitchen window, and as if on cue, a wren burst into song. We had been right to come here after all, I thought.

*　　*　　*

The moon was unearthly bright that night. When I couldn't sleep, I got up and looked out the back bedroom window. I could see the trees' reflection in the river. The shadow of the house lay on the earth, a sharp black triangle, and the pale trees near the cabin were full of shadows. The world outside was an eerie ghost of its day-time self. A light breeze ruffled the curtains at the bedroom windows. Somewhere crickets sang an electric song. Shivering, I slipped back between the sheets. Penn was breathing evenly, his head thrown back so that in the moonlight his throat looked exposed and vulnerable.

I slept fitfully, a thin sleep full of uneasiness. In my dream something was wrong. I was drowning, flailing to get to the air. Then suddenly I awoke with a start, smoke stinging my nostrils. I couldn't make out the outline of the dressing table—only a slight shimmer of its mirror shone in the gray darkness. The room was full of smoke!

"Penn!" I cried. I shook his shoulder, coughing.

When he didn't move at once, cold fear gripped me. "Penn!" I screamed. "The house is on fire!"

I felt him struggle to prop himself on his elbows, coughing.

I pushed him off the bed. "Get down low." I coughed and scrambled off the bed myself, my bare foot tangled in a sheet. With a whimper of panic I tore myself free. "Stay on the floor," I yelled. "There's more air down there." Slithering along the floor, I pressed my palm against the closed door of the bedroom. It was hot. I knew that meant the fire was in the passageway. "We can't get out the door!" I coughed. I couldn't see Penn. The fear flashed through me that he was unconscious somewhere on the floor. How would I find him now in this dark and smoke? And even if I found him, how could I possibly carry him?

The white curtain fluttered ahead of me, a beacon in the smoke. "Joanna!"

My heart gave a thump of relief. "Here I am," I coughed. "I'm coming." A strong hand pulled me toward the window. Dimly I wondered if we should have tried to close the windows. I knew the breeze would fan the fire. But there was no time. We might be overcome by the smoke any minute. I heard a ripping sound, and the curtain rod clattered to the floor. The curtain billowed and swirled over me. Frantically I pushed the soft folds of material away. I heard a crash and a crunching creaking sound and realized Penn was kicking the screen out. Then his hand clasped my arm and he dragged me toward him. I was coughing hard as he lifted me under the arms and thrust my head through the open window. I gasped in the fresh air. Tears streamed down my cheeks, and I snuffled noisily as I struggled to get out. Then I was falling. Sharp branches tore at my arms and legs. I landed with a painful jolt, biting my tongue. "Penn!" I screamed. "Penn!"

A noisy thrashing in the shrubs, and then he was next to me. His hands gripped my forearms only for a minute. "I've got to turn the hose on the house," he said.

My scratched hands and legs were stinging from sweat. When I tried to move, the torn ruffle of my nightgown tripped me. I bent and ripped it off. Then I struggled through the undergrowth. I could hear the whoosh of rushing air and the crackle of flames. When I got to the front of the house, I could see that it was blazing. I could see the fire burning inside through the big plate-glass window. Luridly lit by the flames, Penn stood holding the garden hose, playing a feeble stream of water on the roof. I saw that he had hooked the garden hose up to the freestanding pipe in the front, a remnant of the days before the house had indoor plumbing. I knew it was hopeless. The smell of burning was strong, and I could hear ominous cracking sounds from inside. I suspected that the floor was giving way.

Penn glanced at me. "We'd better stand clear," he said. "The walls might cave in."

I swallowed, hugging myself tightly. "Hadn't we better go for help or something?" I glanced at the Corvette, its red hood gleaming in the firelight. "Do you even have the key to the car?" I gulped. It had just hit me that everything was gone—my duffel bag, the rose chintz chairs. Everything.

The flickering firelight made Penn's bare skin red. The draft from the fire ruffled his short pajama bottoms as he groped under the car. "I keep a spare key on one of those magnet things," he said.

He unlocked the car and I got in. Penn slid in behind the wheel. "I guess we're lucky to be alive," he said in an odd voice. He rested his forehead against the steering wheel a second. Then he lifted his head and started the car. "The nearest fire department is fifteen miles away," he said. "By the time they get here, all that'll be left is a pile of ashes." There was a catch in his voice.

He backed the car out of the driveway and onto the highway, not looking at the burning house.

"The bait shop down the road will have a phone," he said.

I darted a glance at him. The lights of the dash painted a glow on his expressionless face. "But will anyone be there?" I asked. "I mean, isn't the bait shop closed?"

"I think the owner sleeps over the shop," said Penn.

The car's headlights reached into the uncertain darkness. Penn left the windows of the car up as we sped toward the bait shop. I think he was trying to blow away the smell of the fire or perhaps some indefinable danger of the night. But there was no getting away from the smell of the fire. Our clothes stank of it, and the car smelled like—Stephen's car.

"This wasn't an accident, was it?" I said suddenly.

He shrugged.

"We didn't even cook, Penn. We never turned on the stove. We ate cold cuts for lunch and dinner."

"There is such a thing as an electrical fire," he said. I knew he didn't think it was an accident either.

At last the headlights found the crude sign that said BAIT SHOP. Its faded red arrow pointed in the direction of the river. Penn turned, and the car bumped over the rough dirt road. The moonlight showed the woods thick and shadowy around us. Soon the unpainted and decayed old house appeared. It looked like the sort of place that might not even have electricity, much less a phone. The tin roof was silvery in the moonlight, and in the shadows I sensed the presence of porch railings and of smelly wooden boxes where bait was stored. Penn drove close to the shack and stopped the car, leaving his lights shining on the ramshackle porch. He leapt out of the car, and I heard him banging on the door. Its screen rattled.

"Hello?" he called. "Hello up there? Can we use your phone?"

A window was flung open overhead and a stream of obscenities was shouted down at us. "Are you crazy?" yelled the hoarse voice overhead. "It's three in the morning."

Penn stepped away from the door and stood in the headlights so the bait man could see him. "I'm very sorry to bother you," he said, "but we're your neighbors down the way—"

"Yeah, yeah," the man growled. "I can see you."

"And our house is on fire." Penn's voice was

steady. "We only got out with what we were wearing."

"Why didn't you say so!" cried the man. The window slammed shut.

I got out of the car. The gamey smell of bait and crayfish was strong. The crickets, who had gone silent at Penn's shout, resumed singing. A yellow light came on and the screen door of the shack squeaked open. "Get on in," urged the man. "Hurry up. You'll let in the mosquitoes." When I went in, he already had the phone receiver in his hand and was dialing the fire station. He handed it to Penn then, and I heard Penn giving directions to the cabin. We were standing in a small room that was connected to the main part of the shop by an open door. The light from the door showed stacks of inner tubes and slanted bins of fishing tackle.

The bait man was wearing boxer shorts and a sleeveless T-shirt, which revealed a thickness of black hair on his chest as well as a blue and pink tattoo on his withered biceps. His hair was unruly bristles, and his face and arms were browned and weathered so that they scarcely seemed to belong with his spindly white legs.

I was uncomfortably aware of my thin nightgown. Not that the man was looking at me.

"Do you think the fire could spread to the woods, boy?" the man asked anxiously when Penn hung up.

"I can't say, sir," said Penn. "The woods are cleared around the front of the house and we've got the river right behind it, so maybe not."

The man turned on a rusty tap over a big metal sink. This dingy little room must serve as his kitchen. A tiny refrigerator sat near the telephone and a hot plate was on the vinyl counter next to a microwave. "You want some coffee or something?" he asked.

"In a minute, thanks. Right now I'd better call my father and the police."

The man's mouth fell open. "The police?"

"Just in case it wasn't an accident," said Penn. He turned back to the phone.

"Why wouldn't it be an accident?" the bait man asked me excitedly. "What makes anybody think it wasn't an accident?"

I shrugged helplessly. "It happened so fast," I said. "And we hadn't been cooking or anything. Nothing was even turned on."

"These things can start in the walls," said the bait man. "Before you know it, the place is up in smoke. I knew somebody that happened to. They got the cat out, but that was all.

Everything went, even this guy's false teeth."

Penn stretched the cord of the phone out and stepped into the next room to talk. He must be calling his father.

"I don't *know* what happened," I heard him say desperately, his voice raised. "I tell you, we were lucky to get out alive. No, of course I didn't leave anything on the stove. It's three in the morning. What could be on the stove?" He lowered his voice then, and I couldn't make out the words, though I could hear the tense, angry tone.

"You want that coffee now?" the man asked when Penn came back in the room to hang up and redial.

Penn nodded, then stepped back into the next room with the phone.

"I wonder if I'd better wet down my roof or something," said the man nervously. "If it spreads to the woods, this place'll go up like tinder."

"Maybe the fire department can keep the fire from spreading," I said.

My body was still pumping adrenaline, and I was caught up in the immediate emergency, worrying about my nightgown being too thin and about Penn's dad being angry at him. Inconsequential things. It really hadn't quite hit me that the cabin was gone. Finally Penn was off the phone. He automatically took the mug of coffee the man offered him.

We held the hot mugs in both hands and burned our lips on his coffee. Then we thanked the man again for his help and said we'd better be getting back. "I feel like I ought to be there when the fire department comes," explained Penn.

The man shrugged. I'm sure he was thinking, No need to rush. The house is gone. But he didn't say it.

Penn bumped the car slowly off the bait-shop property.

"What did you say to the police?" I asked.

"Not much," he said. "I didn't have to say much."

"What do you mean?" I was straining anxiously to hear his quiet voice.

"They recognized my name," he said.

We drove in silence for a moment, until at last Penn spoke bitterly. "Yeah, they've noticed I've been mixed up in a murder, and maybe it occurred to them that I was a friend of Casey's, who so conveniently committed suicide afterward, and now I tell them I've had a fire at my place. They are very interested."

"Maybe you shouldn't have called them," I said anxiously.

"It doesn't make any difference," he said. "They would come into it anyway. This way, at least it looks like I'm not trying to hide anything."

"How can they tell if it was arson?" I asked.

"The fire starts in several places at once, for one thing. And if somebody has sloshed gasoline all over the place, they can tell that because it leaves a different kind of burn mark or something."

"Do you think that's what it was?"

Penn made a helpless gesture with one hand. "Who knows? My dad is driving out here, by the way." He shook his head.

I gulped. Oddly enough, I was less concerned by my narrow brush with death than by having to meet Penn's father for the first time. The torn nightgown would make a great first impression. I wondered vaguely if I could get a fireman to lend me a raincoat.

Six

Wailing sirens announced the arrival of the fire department. Penn had left the Corvette about twenty feet from the driveway, on the shoulder of the road, in order to give the fire trucks room to turn in. We were standing in front, watching the burning house, when the first of the long red trucks pulled into the driveway. Another followed directly after it. Men wearing shiny raincoats and brimmed helmets and carrying big flashlights leapt off the truck. "We're going to have to get the water out of the river," a fireman told us. "You'd better show us where we can hook up the pump."

Another fireman tossed me a blanket, which I took gratefully and wrapped around myself. Penn led the fireman past the house into the darkness, and in minutes the big canvas hoses filled with water. Firemen stood in front of the house, playing long powerful streams of water onto the roof. The plate-glass window in front had shattered, and only a gaping hole remained where its glassy eye had once looked out on the woods.

Penn came back to stand beside me. "I wonder if they can save anything," he said. "The walls, maybe?" He shivered. "I guess not."

A tall man came up to stand beside me, and with a faint shock I realized he wasn't wearing the regulation black slicker of the fireman. He was holding a soft bundle of some sort and stared as if hypnotized at the burning building. "Hi, Dad," said Penn in a strained voice.

Dr. Parrish stared at the burning building, his face ruddy in the reflected light of the flames. With a start, he seemed to remember Penn. He frowned at him. "I brought you something to wear," he said gruffly, tossing the bundle to Penn. Penn caught it. Quickly he pulled on a sweatshirt and then stepped into the jeans. He handed the extra sweatshirt to me. When I put it on, it came halfway to my knees.

"Have you called your parents, Joanna?" Dr. Parrish asked me.

"N-not yet," I stuttered. My dad had gotten

in the habit of spending the weekends with his girlfriend, and though the number was written down somewhere at home, I didn't know it by heart. If Dr. Parrish imagined my father would be frantic with worry about me, and extremely interested in my narrow escape, he was wrong.

"What happened?" Dr. Parrish asked us.

"I told you what happened," said Penn. "When we woke up, the room was full of smoke. The fire was already in the hall, and we couldn't get out that way, so I kicked out a screen and we got out the window. I tried turning the hose on it, but it was no use."

Dr. Parrish looked at him steadily. "Listen here—you two kids weren't doing something in there that you shouldn't have been, were you?"

I could feel myself going hot all the way down to my toes, as if I had been dipped in boiling water.

"No, Dad," said Penn with a sharp intake of his breath. "We were not freebasing cocaine. Get real."

I stared at Dr. Parrish in amazement. It had never occurred to me that that was what he was hinting at.

"Is that the truth?" he asked me.

"I don't even know what cocaine looks like,"

I said. I had forgotten that Penn's dad had decided Penn must be on drugs when he found out about all the bonds Penn had cashed in. He was so wrong, it was almost funny. Penn hadn't needed the money for drugs—he had needed it to pay off Casey. But he couldn't tell his father that.

Dr. Parrish's gaze was drawn again to the house. I remembered Penn saying that his parents had built the house by hand, doing all the carpentry work themselves in the early, happy days of their marriage. Penn's dad hadn't come out to the cabin much since Penn's mom took off with another man. These days the cabin seemed to belong to Penn. I wondered if Dr. Parrish was sorry to see it burn, or whether he felt a kind of relief. It was impossible to read his face.

"At least you both got out safely," he said at last. "That's the important thing. It's only a house, after all."

The blank look in Penn's eyes as he gazed at the charred timbers told me that he didn't agree. All of his happiest childhood memories were going up in smoke. Suddenly I felt sick with loss. I think for the first time, I had begun to realize that we would not be coming back here.

A dark car pulled up behind the second fire

truck. When the doors opened, I saw that the one nearest me bore the insignia of the police department.

A nearby fireman pushed his helmet up to wipe his brow, and I saw his face was black with ashes and streaked with sweat. "This may be one for you guys," he called to them.

The police officer was wearing an ordinary blue shirt and chinos. If it hadn't been for the official car, I would never have guessed he was a policeman. He went over to the fireman and they stood, heads together, conferring, while the second officer came over to stand with us. He was a thin-lipped man with crinkly, short-cropped dark hair. "Hiya, Doc." He nodded to Penn's father. "So we've got a case of arson, here, huh?"

Penn looked at me helplessly.

"It happened so fast," I explained. "All of a sudden there was fire all over the place, and we couldn't figure out how it could have started."

"Who's got it in for you, son?" The policeman's gaze raked over Penn from head to toe.

"No one that I know of," Penn replied steadily.

"Where's your car?" asked the officer.

Penn jerked his head toward it. "I pulled it off the road so the fire trucks could get in."

"But it was parked out front before?"

Penn nodded.

"If the place went up in flames so fast," said the officer, his eyes narrowing, "how come you had your car keys?"

"I keep a spare in one of those magnet cases under the car," said Penn.

"Bad idea," said the officer. "Somebody could steal your car real easy that way."

"It was just as well, though, wasn't it?" said Dr. Parrish. "Since he had to go for help."

I knew that Penn and his father had their problems with each other. It was interesting to watch them close ranks against a common enemy.

The officer shot Penn's father a nasty look. "Your son is having an awful lot of bad luck, isn't he, sir? One of his friends is murdered. Then another one commits suicide. And now somebody's tried to burn his house down with him in it."

"That remains to be seen," retorted Dr. Parrish. "The fire could be accidental."

But the other officer was already walking toward us, nodding. "The fire chief thinks it's arson," he said when he reached us.

"Look, Officer," Dr. Parrish said. "My son and this young lady are in shock. I think you'd better delay your questioning until they have a chance to pull themselves together. I want to get them on home."

Penn's father walked with us to the car. "Are you okay to drive?" Dr. Parrish asked Penn in an urgent voice.

"Yeah," said Penn. "I don't want to leave the 'Vette out here all night. I'll drive it."

We got in the Corvette together and drove off, leaving the house smoldering behind us. As we drove down the highway, I spotted Dr. Parrish's Continental in the rearview mirror. He was following us at a distance. I wasn't sure whether he was afraid Penn was going to pass out behind the wheel or what.

"Whew!" I said, leaning back in the bucket seat. "That policeman was scary!"

The woods on either side of the road looked washed out in the moonlight. Our headlights turned the yellow stripes at the side of the road to glitter. Penn turned on the windshield wipers, and they made a clear path on the deeply slanted glass. At first I thought they were brushing away tree pollen, but then I saw crusty gray bits at the edge and realized the windshield was covered with ashes.

The cabin was gone, I remembered, and a lump rose in my throat.

Penn licked his lips. "You realize that's not the last we're going to be hearing from the cops, don't you? You heard them."

"Oh, Penn, they can't believe you set that fire!"

"Yeah, but it looks fishy. Did you hear them say I'm 'unlucky'?"

"People do have bad luck," I suggested. "They don't get sent to jail for it."

"You know who gets their houses set on fire?" Penn asked. "Drug kingpins, that's who. And sleazy types messed up in insurance fraud."

"That doesn't make any sense," I argued. "If you were selling drugs, you'd be making money, right? Not cashing in those bonds your grandmother gave you for college."

"Don't remind me," groaned Penn. "All I need is for them to talk to the nosy teller who told my dad I was cashing in those bonds."

The missing money did look bad, I had to admit that. Penn couldn't account for what had happened to it without giving away that Casey had been blackmailing him. And if the police somehow found out about all the money that had gone to Casey, it was going to look very bad. "I don't think your father is going to tell them about it," I said. "He's on your side. You saw the way he was just now."

Penn snorted. "I never figured he wanted to see me tried and convicted of murder, Joanna. But that doesn't make him any hero."

I glanced at him. "He sort of sounds like you, you know?"

"I don't want to hear it," Penn said tightly. "I'm not a bit like him. It's purely an accident of biology that we're related." I had been surprised to find I liked Penn's dad. I suppose in small ways he reminded me of Penn, and I liked the way he had jumped to Penn's defense.

Dear Diary,

I'm back in my own bedroom now, but the smell of smoke clings to my hair, and I can't forget the sight of the flames leaping inside the cabin. What if I hadn't woken up? What if we had been overcome by smoke before we could get out of the bedroom?

I've wadded up my torn nightgown and stuffed it in the trash. I don't want a souvenir of this scary night. Even the lingering faint smell of smoke makes me shiver. Our charred bodies could have been pulled out of the wreckage by the firefighters. Stephen had tried to kill us!

Seven

. . . I washed the smell of smoke out of my hair last night, but it didn't erase the memory of the fire. I'm still shivering with fear. I was woken up this morning by a call from the police. They want me to come to the station at one o'clock to answer some questions, but I can't seem to get out of bed. I'm so scared! I'm lying here with the shades drawn, trying to shake the feeling that Stephen is lying in wait for me outside. The simplest daily routines—driving to school, walking by an open window—suddenly seem risky. I think of the blank look on Casey's slack face, and I feel cold inside. That could be me. Dead. Nowhere is safe.

The phone rang, and I reached for it with an unsteady hand.

"Joanna?"

"Penn!" It was so good to hear his voice, I felt weak with relief. Somehow I felt Penn could make everything all right.

"I was afraid I might wake you up. Have you had breakfast?" he asked.

"No." I paused. "I haven't gotten around to eating yet," I said. I didn't want him to know how scared I was. He would only blame himself for putting me in danger.

"Why don't I come pick you up and we'll go get breakfast, then?"

"That sounds great." All I could think of was that if Penn could put his arms around me, I would feel safe.

"Joanna—" He hesitated, "Watch for me, and when you see my car pull up to the driveway, run out as fast as you can. I mean, when you come out that door, keep right on moving."

"You don't seriously think Stephen has a rifle pointed at my door, do you?" A chill ran down my back.

"No. He can't. For one thing, he's scared of Bobby, so Bobby's living right across the street is good insurance. The last thing Stephen wants is for Bobby to catch him slinking around your neighborhood with a rifle."

Penn was right. I could easily imagine Bobby banging Stephen on the head with the butt of his own rifle.

"I figure it's better for us to get in the habit of not being sitting ducks, if you get my drift," Penn went on.

After we hung up, I jumped up and pulled on jeans and a shirt. It had been a mistake to lie in bed so long. I had to go on with my life, do normal things, or I was going to completely lose it.

I watched from the window in the living room until I saw Penn's car. The door flew open. Then I ran down the steps and slid in. "So far, so good," I said.

We ended up going to Flannigan's Family Restaurant. It was full of booster chairs and squalling toddlers. We hadn't been there before because we weren't much interested in getting a balloon with Chicky the Clown's picture on it. But Flannigan's had the advantage of having a number of inside booths that were well away from the windows, out of the reach of gunfire. That was all that seemed to matter to us right now.

"Dad drove out this morning to look at the

cabin," said Penn after we ordered. "The outside walls are still standing. He said it was eerie, like a ghost house."

"You didn't go along with him?"

Penn winced. "I couldn't. I just couldn't." He shook his head. "What Dad's worried about is his liability." Penn's voice was resentful. "He's afraid the walls'll fall on somebody and he'll get sued. He's already talked to somebody about getting them torn down.

"The floor had collapsed in most of the house," said Penn, "but the bedroom was pretty much intact, and he rescued a few things." Penn laid my wallet on the table, the thin, men's wallet I carried because it fit better in jeans. At least I don't have to get a new driver's license now, I thought, opening it up. But catching a whiff of smoke, I closed it hastily and tucked it away. I was glad I hadn't taken my diary with me to the cabin. The truth was I didn't like Penn to know I was still writing in my diary, since it had already gotten us in so much trouble.

"I called my mother first thing this morning," Penn said, "but all I got was her answering machine, so we can't go there. I don't even have a key. She and my stepfather must be out of town."

I knew it would have been safer to stay with

Penn's mother's in Maryland. But when I thought of meeting her and facing her curiosity about me and my family, my heart failed me. She would wonder what Penn saw in me. Worse, she would wonder why I wasn't staying with my own mother, and my mother was something I definitely didn't want to talk about.

The waitress brought our order, and Penn waited until she was out of earshot before he spoke.

"I'm supposed to go in and talk to the police this afternoon," he said. "They called me this morning."

"Me too," I said.

Penn's eyes widened. "You?"

"I was there, you know," I said. "I'm a witness, the same as you are."

"I hate it that you're mixed up in this," Penn said. His eyes were smoldering. I knew that he was angry about a lot of things he couldn't do anything about—Stephen burning up the cabin, Casey blackmailing him, Laurie's death. He was probably even mad that his mother was out of town when he needed her.

"Penn," I said hesitantly. "Couldn't we hint to the police that Stephen might have done it? Just think—if they lock Stephen up, we'll be safe!"

"Are you out of your mind?" he asked. "If they arrest him, he'll take us down with him. He'd make damn sure I never drew a free breath."

"I don't see how we'd be worse off than we are now," I insisted stubbornly. "Don't you think we might be better off to tell the police the whole truth? I mean about Laurie and Casey—everything?"

He stared at me in horror. "Don't even think about it!" He glanced around to make sure no one was close enough to hear, then leaned over toward me, his face pale. "If I tell the police Stephen pushed Laurie over the cliff, all he has to do is tell them that I was the one who did the pushing."

"But he couldn't do that!" I gasped. "Tessa . . ." My voice trailed off.

"Right," said Penn. "See what I'm saying? With Casey gone, Tessa's the only other witness to what happened. And who do you think Tessa would want to have put in jail for twenty years—me, or Stephen?"

"She wouldn't." But suddenly I wasn't sure. I knew we couldn't risk it.

At one o'clock I was going to have to go in and lie to the police. I would have to tell them I had no idea why anybody would want to kill us. None.

I found myself mentally groping for a way out. Could there be any chance that the fire would turn out to be caused by a short in the electrical system after all? "Penn, the person who called me from the police station didn't say much. Are they absolutely sure it was arson?"

Penn nodded. "When they called this morning, they said they had recovered some kerosene-soaked rags."

A waitress walked by us, carrying a bunch of helium balloons.

"Stephen must have gotten in the crawl space and spread out a bunch of rags and kerosene," said Penn, following the waitress with his eyes.

"It's so weird," I whispered. "I can't quite picture it. I mean, I can't picture Stephen——"

Penn stabbed at his plate with his fork. "I know. I've been over and over that myself. You can imagine how it makes me feel when my best friend tries to fry me," he said bitterly. "Either he's a psychopath and I never knew it, or else deep down inside he hates me and I never suspected. Whichever way you look at it, I come out looking pretty dumb."

"Maybe he didn't really mean to kill us, Penn. Maybe he was only trying to scare us and the fire got out of control."

Penn laughed shortly. "Sure."

In a nearby booth a child burst into tears. His helium balloon had floated up to the ceiling, out of his reach. The lost pink balloon clung to the ceiling as if it had been nailed there. The child bawled.

"I just wish I knew what he was going to try next," said Penn.

I arrived at the police station at one. The station was a part of the big city hall. Police cars were parked along the curb in front of the station, and on either side of the entrance stood a pair of glass globes labeled POLICE.

When I pushed open the glass door and went in, I saw a row of chairs lined up against the wall. Penn was sitting in one and smiling at me. A uniformed woman, looking thoroughly bored, waved me toward the chairs. I sat down next to Penn and crossed my ankles primly.

"Are you in disguise or what?" asked Penn, eyeing me curiously.

I glanced down self-consciously at my navy skirt and white blouse. My tastes generally ran to jeans and loosely woven shirts. My favorite earrings were dangling little bells that I had picked up at a Grateful Dead concert, but today I was wearing simple gold studs instead. "I wanted to look respectable," I explained.

Penn glanced furtively toward the uniformed lady. She was sitting behind a kind of raised counter. "Aren't you surprised they had us both come in at the same time?" Penn asked.

"Maybe we'll go in separately," I said.

After a few minutes, though, a uniformed officer asked for us both to follow him. The police officer ushered us into a room with a long table. Sitting at it was the dark-haired man who had come to the fire the night before. His jaws were faintly blue. I supposed he was one of those men who would have to shave twice a day to look clean shaven. His closely waved hair gleamed under the fluorescent light, and his lips were pressed together in a thin line.

"Well, well, well," he said. "Sit down. Have a seat." He smiled grimly. "My name is Lieutenant Strickland, by the way."

I pulled a chair out with a deafening screech and sat down. Penn sat next to me. Under the table I felt his warm hand, reassuringly on my knee.

"You two over the scare you had last night?" the policeman asked.

"I guess we're still a little shaken up," said Penn, answering for both of us.

"Kind of a close call," said the officer. "You were real lucky. Smoke inhalation is a bad business." His bright eyes darted quickly first to one of us, then the other. "What happened that made you wake up? Did you hear a noise?"

"I was having a bad dream," I said. "About choking. I guess it was the smoke that woke me up."

A blond man quietly slipped into the room and sat down. He was slender and his hair was close-cropped.

"I asked Captain Kronkie from homicide to sit in today," said the other officer smoothly. "Since this arson might tie in with a case he's working on. Let's see, you were just explaining that you think a bad dream woke you up. Then what?"

"Then I woke Penn up," I said.

"You sleep in the same bed?" Lieutenant Strickland asked mildly.

I could feel myself going scarlet.

"Yes," Penn put in. He regarded the lieutenant coolly. "Joanna's a lighter sleeper than I am."

"There was a bright moon," I said. "I always have trouble sleeping when there's a full moon."

"Interesting." Lieutenant Strickland scribbled something on a legal pad. "I've heard that dogs howl at the full moon, but I never heard it causes insomnia. So you didn't hear anything, am I right?"

"No," I said. "Nothing. I woke up and then I realized there was smoke in the room. Usually I can see the mirror across from the bed—it catches the light. But I couldn't make it out. And then I smelled the smoke."

"What time was that?" the blond man said, and I jumped at the unexpected sound of his voice.

"It must have been not long before three," Penn said. "I'm not sure how long it took us to get out the window—not long. I tried to turn the garden hose on the fire, but pretty soon I saw that that wasn't helping. So probably it didn't take more than a half hour from the time we climbed out the window to the time we were banging on the door of the bait shop."

Lieutenant Strickland consulted his notes. "The call came in at five after three," he said.

"What possible difference can it make?" I put in.

The lieutenant regarded me blandly. "We're trying to establish the time of the crime."

Crime. The word rang uncomfortably in my ears, and I sat back in my chair, hoping I didn't look as guilty as I felt.

"Even with the large amount of combustible

material used, it might have taken as much as an hour, even more, for the fire to get as far as it did before you woke up. I understand you climbed out the window because the fire was already in the hall." Lieutenant Strickland shot me a glance. "Do you usually sleep with the door closed?"

"Yes," said Penn.

"Yet no one else was at the cabin with you?" The lieutenant narrowed his eyes.

"It's a habit," said Penn.

"More often we go to the cabin with a group of friends," I explained, but as soon as I had spoken, I wished I hadn't.

"Oh?" inquired the lieutenant. "And why didn't your friends join you on this occasion?"

"They were taking the A.P. tests," I said.

"The Advanced Placement tests," Penn explained. "For college credit."

"Now, let's see," said the lieutenant. "Those friends would be . . ."

"Tessa West and Stephen Garner," supplied the blond officer in a dry voice. "Your friends are thinning out fast, aren't they, Parrish? Weren't Laurie Jenkins and Casey MacNamara friends of yours?"

"Yes," said Penn. His face was expressionless,

and with alarm I saw why Captain Kronkie would be suspicious of Penn. He looked as if he was hiding something.

"Can you explain why such a string of bad luck has come your way?" asked Captain Kronkie.

"Casey killed himself because he was depressed," I put in quickly. "Everyone knew that. And maybe Laurie's death was one of the reasons he was depressed. So it was like one thing led to another. Laurie's death could have been part of the cause of Casey's death." I could feel my face growing hot. Laurie's death was connected to Casey's, but not that way. I wished I were more used to telling lies.

"But the fire." Captain Kronkie tapped his pencil eraser absently on the table. "How can you explain that?"

"I can't," Penn said flatly. "I don't know what happened."

"I understand the structure was insured," said Lieutenant Strickland.

I stared at him, astonished that he might seriously think Penn would burn down the cabin to collect insurance money. "Penn loved that cabin!" I exclaimed. "He would never have burned it down."

"Besides, how could he?" The lieutenant smiled. "He was in bed with you, right?"

I went rigid and closed my mouth firmly, afraid of what I might say.

"Any insurance money would go to my father," said Penn stiffly. "And my father isn't in desperate need of money, you know."

"Right. I know that." The lieutenant looked up from his notes. "Nice car you've got, by the way, son."

To me the questioning seemed unreal. Sleeping together and having a nice car weren't crimes, but the lieutenant's conviction that they were seemed to underlie the line of questioning.

"Do you have any idea," asked Lieutenant Strickland, "who might have set this fire? Anyone who holds a grudge, anyone who is afraid of you?"

At his last words I blinked guiltily. Stephen was afraid of us. He was afraid we were going to talk to the police. I wondered if he had followed us here and was waiting outside.

"No idea at all," said Penn firmly.

Lieutenant Strickland asked us more questions after that. Were rags stored under the house? Was kerosene kept on the premises? Had we noticed anyone hanging about the place?

Any petty thievery? Any sign of squatters using the cabin when we weren't there?

Captain Kronkie didn't say much, and when he did speak, his questions were absentminded. He obviously thought there was some connection between the deaths of our friends and the fire. But he seemed to be in no big hurry to find out what the connection was. It was almost as if he felt the answer was going to fall into his lap.

As we got up to leave, Kronkie tapped his pencil on the table. "You almost got yourselves killed, you realize," he said slowly. His eyes met Penn's. "The next time you may not be so lucky. It's to your advantage to talk to us. Think it over."

Penn and I looked at him blankly, then turned and left the room. We walked together out to our cars. I groped in my pocketbook for a tissue and blew my nose. "That Captain Kronkie is awful. He gives me the creeps," I said.

Penn opened the car door for me. "Yeah. He's the one I told you about, remember? The one who doesn't like me."

"He sounded almost as if he knew what was going on," I said.

"Believe me, if he knew what was going on," said Penn, "he wouldn't have let us walk out of there."

I squinted against the sun as I got in. "Penn, did you have the feeling Kronkie is waiting for something?"

"You mean some report? Like from a wiretap, or from somebody following us? Something like that?"

"I don't know—I guess I expected him to push us more for answers."

"Sorry to disappoint you, but they don't allow the police to use rubber hoses anymore." Penn slammed the door shut.

. . . Funny how my interest in telling the police the whole story dried up once I got to the police station. That oily smile of Lieutenant Strickland's and the cold blue gaze of Captain Kronkie froze my blood. These men are my enemies. In a moment of insane optimism, I had hoped they would be as warm and understanding as the loving father I never had. But now I know I can't trust them. Penn and I are in this by ourselves.

Eight

Dear Diary,

It's strange to wake up in my own bed and find Penn asleep beside me. His face is flushed; his hair is messy and slightly damp with sweat. Having him stay over, here in my father's house, feels faintly illicit. But we can't go to the cabin anymore, because the cabin is gone. If we have to wait in fear for Stephen's next move, our hearts pounding, then at least we can sleep in each other's arms.

Penn groaned and stretched until one bare foot popped out from under the sheet. I laid my diary on the floor and snuggled up next to him, my head in the hollow of his crooked arm.

"Mmm," he said, landing a kiss on the top of my head. "Jeez, look at the time!"

I saw by the alarm clock that it was almost noon.

Penn slid quickly out of bed. He pulled a comb through his hair and hastily pulled on jeans and a T-shirt. "I'm not crazy about the idea of bumping into your dad," he said. "What time do you think he'll get home?"

"I can't ever tell. Sometimes he comes in early, sometimes not."

I tugged the blinds open and the room was flooded with light. The sun blazed a golden path on the pond outside. "What do we do next, Penn?" I perched on my knees on the bed. "Do we go to school tomorrow or what?"

Penn was brushing his teeth, and he looked comical with foam bubbling out of his mouth.

I sighed. "I love to watch you," I said.

He wiped his mouth and grinned at me. "You are out of your mind."

"I love you, that's all," I said. I got off the bed and went over to him. He put his arms around me, and my cheek pressed against the damp flesh of his chest.

"I guess we go to school as if nothing has happened," he said. "I don't think the cops would like it if we stopped going. It would look awfully funny if we dropped out just before graduation."

"I don't see what difference it would make. They couldn't be any more suspicious of us than they are now," I said. "But I guess we have to go to school." I shook my hair off my shoulders. "I'll go crazy if I have to sit around the house all day by myself."

Penn grinned. "Hey, another murder attempt, no big deal. Nothing scares us, right?"

Just for the moment, I felt both brave and lucky. We had escaped the fire. Why couldn't we escape the next thing Stephen tried? "We'll have to be careful, though," I said, cautioning myself.

"Right." Penn glanced at the clock. "Well, look, I'd better go."

We were kissing good-bye in the living room when suddenly the front door opened and my father stepped in. For a moment my father and Penn stared into each other's eyes.

"Hello," my father said.

"Hi," said Penn. "Well, I'll be seeing you, Joanna."

My father stepped aside. Penn squeezed by him, then turned around as soon as he got out on the front porch. The bright sun picked out the platinum strands in his hair and cast his eyes into shadow. He flashed me a smile. "Talk to you later."

My father's hostile gaze followed him as he walked out to his Corvette. The low red car pulled away. "I hope the boyfriend's not planning on moving in." My father at last closed the door and turned to look at me, frowning. He tossed the Sunday paper onto the couch.

"He only stayed over because I was so shaken up, I was afraid to be alone." I confronted him defiantly, my feet apart, my arms folded. "Penn's cabin burned down Friday night. The police said we were lucky to get out alive."

"The police?" My father's voice was sharp. "How do the police come into it?"

I stared at him a moment. I had been so keen to put my father on the defensive that I hadn't chosen my words with enough care. I shouldn't have mentioned the police, I realized. The last thing I wanted was for him to get curious about my life all of a sudden, when I had so much to hide. "Oh, I guess they have to investigate all unexplained fires," I said, turning away.

"First I've heard of it," my father said. "You say it happened Friday? Was it written up in the paper?"

I shrugged. "Probably not. Nobody was hurt,

after all." I took a deep breath. Change the subject, I told myself. He's not really interested. "So how's Jennifer getting along?" I asked.

"Fine," said my father. "She's having a lot of trouble with office politics and thinks she's coming down with a head cold. Now, about this fire—you kids didn't leave a pot on the stove or something, did you?"

I shook my head.

"Smoking in bed?" he ventured.

"I think it must have been an electrical short," I said. "Have you had lunch yet?"

"Grabbed a bite at Jen's. Don't worry about me." He hoisted his weekend bag and headed back toward his room.

I won't worry about you, I thought grimly as he went into his room, any more than you worry about me.

After his door closed, I opened the newspaper and leafed through it. It didn't take me long to find the story.

FIRE CLAIMS COUNTRY HOME
ARSON SUSPECTED

The riverfront cabin of Dr. Benjamin Parrish was declared a total loss after a fire Friday night. According to a

police spokesman, arson is suspected. Dr. Parrish's son, Penn, 18,
and a guest who was also staying at
the cabin escaped without injury.
Two trucks from the Sunnyside Fire
Department responded to the 3:05
A.M. call. Fire Chief Obie Dennison
told the *Telegram* that a number of
rags soaked in kerosene were recovered from the crawl space of the
house and that the fire had started
in several places at once, indications
of arson. The police are investigat-
ing. The house and its contents were
valued at $60,000.

I slid the page containing the story out of the
paper, crumbled it up into a ball, and put it at
the bottom of the wastepaper basket where my
father wouldn't see it. Then I refolded the paper
neatly and left it on the kitchen table. Unless he
checked carefully, he would never realize a page
was missing.

When I got to school Monday morning, I was
aware that I wasn't behaving normally. For one
thing, I didn't dare go by my locker for fear I

would run into my lockermate, Koo Ambler, Casey's old girlfriend. To other people Koo must have looked like an ordinary girl in black combat boots who wore too much makeup, but to me she was a spy who might pick up the vibrations of my fear. She and Bobby were friendly, and I was afraid of what might happen if they put their heads together and pooled their information. It was better for me to stay away from her and not risk making her suspicious. I could take all my books home with me every night, I decided, and give up using my locker entirely. Another thing—I took the long way to homeroom, going around the administration building to avoid the dark stairwell where Stephen and Tessa liked to make out.

When I spotted Nikki Warren coming down the hall, I stepped quickly into the girls' bathroom. I knew Nikki was taking up a collection for a memorial to Laurie and Casey, and having to decide on the right amount to give her was more than I could handle. I stood just inside the door and counted to a hundred while I listened to the toilets flush. My face in the mirror looked alarmingly strange. My mouth was working, and I was blinking too much. A girl who stopped at the mirror to put on lipstick shot me a curious look. I hastily pulled out a comb and ran it a few times through my hair. Then I darted out of the bathroom. No sign of Nikki Warren. I breathed a sigh of relief.

Suddenly, without warning, Stephen and Tessa rounded the corner of the hallway. It was too late for me to get away. Tessa rushed up to me and threw her arms around me. "Joanna!" She backed away from me, her dark eyes sparkling with tears. "It's too awful!" she cried. "Is the cabin really gone?"

I nodded, unable to speak.

"I didn't see the paper until this morning. I could hardly believe it!" she said. "It's horrible!"

"Sounds like you and Penn had a close call," said Stephen. "You were lucky not to get caught in the house."

My eyes darted anxiously to his face. Couldn't Tessa hear the threat underneath his words? He was warning me that I wouldn't be so lucky next time.

"It scares me to think about it," cried Tessa. "The house doesn't matter. I mean, of course it matters, but Stephen's right. The big thing is that you and Penn got out okay. Why didn't you call us and tell us what happened? We were out of the A.P. tests by three."

"I guess we were both pretty shook up." I hesitated. "And then Saturday afternoon we had to go in and talk to the police."

Stephen stiffened. "The police? Why?"

I squirmed under his gaze. "The police think it was arson," I said. "That's why they wanted to ask us some questions."

"That's what it said in the paper." Tessa lowered her voice. "Someone set the fire on purpose! I've thought about it and thought about it, and do you know what I've decided? It must have been Bobby!"

"Bobby?" I was caught for the moment off balance.

"Don't you think?" Tessa asked excitedly. "You know he never did like any of us. He was always getting in digs about us to Laurie."

"Joanna is probably thinking that you don't kill people just because you don't like them," said Stephen, amused.

I wondered if I had ever really known him at all. And then, all of a sudden, Penn was beside me. He threw an arm around me. "Tessa read about the cabin burning in the paper," I explained.

"It was quite a fire," said Penn. I could hear the anger in his voice. "The cabin was a total loss." I put my arm around his waist. I was afraid he would go for Stephen's throat.

"Tell Penn what I said, Joanna," said Tessa urgently.

"Tessa thinks Bobby did it," I said.

"You know," said Tessa, "he's always said he would get back at whoever killed Laurie."

"It's an idea," Penn said, gritting his teeth.

"We're going to have to be very careful from now on!" Tessa said earnestly.

"That's what Joanna and I have been telling ourselves." Penn looked at Stephen squarely. "There's no telling what could happen next."

The bell rang, but for a moment none of us moved.

"You guys!" Nikki Warren swooped down on us. "I'm taking up a collection for a memorial for Casey and Laurie," she said, "and I know you guys will want to contribute."

Traffic surged around us in the hallway, but we all reached at once for our wallets. I stuffed a bill into Nikki's hand.

"Gee, you guys," I heard her say as I hurried off. "This is really generous of you! Honestly!"

Had I given Nikki a one or a twenty? I wondered in a panic. I wasn't even sure. That was guilt at work. The breeze beat against my hot

cheeks as I rushed to my classroom. I only
wanted to get away from Nikki and forget about
her collection to honor the dead. But just as I
got to my classroom, I stopped abruptly in my
tracks. The boy behind me ran right into me.

"Oops!" he said. "Are you all right?"

I stared at him. "I'm fine," I said. It had suddenly hit me that the way I had dressed when I
went to the police station was exactly the way
Nikki Warren did. I must have unconsciously
wanted to imitate her. Maybe once I had
thought her earnestness was a little bit funny,
but not anymore. I only wished I had her clear
conscience.

After third period, Penn was waiting for me
outside my English class. His next class was in
the other wing, so it wasn't as if it was con-
venient for him to come by. I was startled to see
him. "Meet me by the administration building at
lunch," he said breathlessly. "We'll go to a fast-
food place or something."

"Okay," I said. I was thankful that at least I
didn't have to eat lunch with Stephen and Tessa.
Students weren't supposed to go off campus for
lunch, but these days I wasn't worried about
minor infractions of the rules.

*   *   *

Twelve thirty found Penn sitting across from me at a tiny table at Sit 'n' Snack and lathering mustard on his hamburger. We seemed to be living our lives in restaurants. "Can you believe Stephen?" he growled. "Cool as can be. I felt like strangling him."

"Don't even think about it, Penn!" I pleaded. "You know what a temper he's got."

"I'd much rather fight it out with him face-to-face than sneak around waiting for him to shoot us in the back."

"But, Penn," I protested. "What if he doesn't fight back? What if he decides to go to the police and tell them lies about you? Besides, if you and Stephen got in a fight, how would you explain it? People would be bound to wonder. The police might even find out about it and drag you both in for more questioning."

He heaved a sigh. "The whole situation is so crazy, I don't know what makes sense anymore. Half the time I feel like going for Stephen's throat and half the time I feel like running." He grabbed both my hands. "We could sell both our cars and take a train west. Then we could get jobs washing dishes or house-sitting or something."

"We'd have to give our Social Security numbers." I wrested my hands away from him. "We'd need driver's licenses, birth certificates, things like that."

"We could manage somehow," argued Penn. "We could check microfilms of old newspapers until we found death notices for some babies born about when we were born. Then we could send off for the birth certificates, and invent new identities—new Social Security cards, new driver's licenses."

"You mean take the driver's test again?" I asked in a small voice.

Penn laughed. "You crack me up, Joanna. What's taking the driver's test against the choice of either going to jail or getting killed?"

He was right. I was crazy to worry about something so small. But I was right, too. Sometimes it was the small things that were the worst. In a way, meeting Penn's father was more scary than dodging Stephen's bullets. That my nightgown was torn and thin had really been more immediately upsetting than the cabin's burning down. And right now it seemed as if the most difficult part of starting a new life was having to take the driver's test all over again.

The door of the restaurant opened and a plump woman came in carrying an infant seat. Two cute little kids in overalls, maybe four and three years old, were hanging on to her. Penn glanced at them briefly and then turned back to me. "The only thing is, we'd be running the rest of our lives. If we take off like that, it's a confession of murder. I bet Captain Kronkie wouldn't waste any time putting out warrants for our arrests. And if he was too stupid to draw the obvious conclusion, I bet Stephen would give him a hint."

I hadn't touched my hamburger. "We don't have to decide right now," I said.

When we left the restaurant, we passed a newspaper vending machine. Sixties Radical Fugitive Turns Self In. Penn stared at it a moment, then dropped in a quarter and took a paper.

"Hoping to pick up some hints for life on the lam?" I asked lightly.

He didn't answer. After we got in the car, he said, "This afternoon I've got to drive to Greensboro to that drug clinic to get tested. My dad thinks I need help. There's nothing I can do about it. I've got to go."

"I hope the police don't find out," I said. "Something tells me Captain Kronkie would gobble up that information like raw meat."

"I'm sure not going to send them an engraved announcement," said Penn.

I glanced at the speedometer as we cruised down the street. Penn was driving slowly. As long as I had known him, I had wished he would slow down, but now somehow his going under the speed limit bothered me. I realized that he was already practicing for life as a fugitive from justice.

"I feel like everything's closing in on me," he said. "The police are on my tail, Stephen's stalking me, and my dad's watching me. The only question is who's going to get me first."

"Maybe it'll all blow over somehow," I said hopefully.

Penn burst into laughter.

I pressed my fingers against my temples. "Okay, I know I must sound stupid, but I have to keep some optimism going inside me or I'm going to fall to pieces."

"It could be worse." Penn squeezed my knee. "At least we're in this together."

The newspaper lay between our seats. Sixties Radical Fugitive Gives Self Up, blared the headline. Below it was a picture of the radical as a smiling young person about our age with a strong chin and granny glasses. Also her recent mug shot. In the mug shot she had numbers hung around her neck; her hair was stringy and her smile was gone.

. . . *What would it be like to take new names and go far away where no one knew us? Would it be so hard, really? It's not as if I'm close to my father or my mother. It's not as if I have a circle of close friends. No one in this town would even miss me. So why do I shrink from the idea? Why did I say, "We don't have to decide now," hoping that Penn would drop the subject?*

Nine

Dear Diary,

I can't stop thinking about what Penn said. Running away. A new life. Already, since my parents' divorce, I've been to four schools in three years. Penn doesn't know how hard it is. He's lived in the same town his entire life. I never quite remember the way to the dry cleaner's or which streets are one way. It's hard to live with the uneasy feeling of always being a stranger—the cold looks, the unfamiliar faces. I'm not sure I can face it again. I don't have what it takes to keep running the rest of my life.

Clouds hung low and heavy, obscuring the sky; a sultry electric feeling hung in the air.

When the final bell rang to signal school was over, I was in a daze. I moved through the crowded hall, pushing my way past laughing kids without seeing them. What was I going to say if Penn told me he wanted to leave town tonight?

Standing by my car was a kid wearing a baseball cap turned backward and faded jeans. A freckled boy was talking to him, sniffling and wiping his nose with the back of his hand. They moved away hastily when I revved up the engine. When I pulled out of the lot, I swiveled around and saw that Penn's Corvette was almost bumper to bumper with my car. I didn't honk at him, or even smile.

I was driving along the road in front of the school, slowing down, getting ready to brake at the stop sign, when suddenly there was a flash of light, and a huge noise struck me in the face like a blow. It was as if a thunderbolt had hit the car. I cringed against the seat cushion, and the car swerved. The windshield shattered into a spiderweb of cracks, and only sheer reflex made my foot hit the brake.

The car skidded to a stop. Stunned, I looked around and realized that I was in the wrong lane. The car sat crosswise over the center line. Trembling, I got out to check the damage. The bumper of my car was pressed against the bumper of a Mazda in the other lane, but there were no dents that I could see.

Penn ran over to me, kicking up dust as he skidded to a stop. "Are you all right?"

I opened my mouth, but nothing came out.

The door of the Mazda opened and Mr. Dockerty, the physics teacher, got out of it. "What happened?" he asked. "What was that noise?" He pushed his glasses back up on his nose and peered at my car with pale, lashless eyes.

I glanced up at the overcast sky. "It sounded like thunder. Lightning must have struck right next to us."

"Lightning? I think not," he snorted. "Lightning wouldn't have done that to your windshield." He pointed an accusing finger at my car.

Following his gaze, I saw that the spiderweb cracks in my windshield radiated from a single neat round hole.

"A rifle shot," said Penn in an odd voice.

"It does look like a bullet hole," agreed Mr. Dockerty.

"Couldn't sound waves do that," I argued, "if the sound was loud enough? I've heard of greenhouses getting broken by sonic booms."

Mr. Dockerty briefly regarded me with pity. "These hunters," he complained. "When you've got guns that shoot farther than anybody can see, you've got to expect accidents like this." Lightning flashed to the north, and in the distance thunder rumbled. "I doubt if it's going to be possible to track down whoever was so careless," he went on, "but we're going to have to notify the police anyway."

A fresh breeze raised the fine hairs on the back of my neck, and I shivered.

Penn and Mr. Dockerty went around to the other side of the car to get a closer look at the bullet hole.

"You had a close call, young lady," said Mr. Dockerty.

The bullet hole had come in on the passenger side, about an arm's length from my head. I noticed then that a crowd of kids had gathered around. A woman from a nearby house offered to call the police.

I sat down in my car, dangling my legs out the open door, while Penn and Mr. Dockerty speculated about where the bullet came from. A few drops of rain splattered noisily on the hood.

At last the police arrived and dug the bullet out of the seat cushion. I stared at it, stupefied.

"Hey!" a voice called. A uniformed officer stood up suddenly beside a thick stand of young dogwoods just short of the stop sign. "Come here! I think we've got something over here."

I got out of the car and followed the second police officer over to the clump of dogwoods. The other officer pushed aside some leaves, and I saw he was pointing at three indentations on the ground. "Whoever it was, he used a tripod," he commented. "He must have waited right here for you to come along."

Mr. Dockerty blanched. "Do you think he was aiming at me?"

"It's hard to say, sir," said the officer. "That big clap of thunder probably threw him off."

Mr. Dockerty pressed his hand to his chest. "I think I'd better sit down," he said.

The officer bent and picked up a cigarette butt off the dirt. "Looks like he was smoking while he waited."

Penn squeezed my hand. Stephen was a chain-smoker. Neither of us believed that the sniper was gunning for Mr. Dockerty. A cold drop landed on my head. Raindrops rattled softly on the leaves of the dogwoods.

"I've put in a call to homicide," said the officer. "Captain Kronkie is on his way over here."

Two officers strung a yellow tape around the dogwoods. CRIME SCENE—DO NOT CROSS, it said. One of them spread a piece of plastic sheeting over the tripod marks to protect them from the rain.

"Used to be," one of them said, "that we never got a call out here at the high school, but lately it seems like we're out here all the time. It's a regular crime wave."

"Can we go home now?" I asked. Mr. Dockerty had taken refuge in his car, and I was beginning to think I would like to do that, too. My knees felt weak.

"You're not driving your car anywhere until you get the windshield fixed," said one of the cops.

"You'd better wait around in case Captain Kronkie wants to talk to you," added the other.

Penn and I walked back to my car. "Captain Kronkie," said Penn. "Great. Just who we want to see."

I sat down behind the wheel, letting my legs dangle outside. Raindrops pattered lightly on my shoes, leaving shiny spatter marks. Penn's shirt was streaked from the rain. "Penn?" I gazed up at him. "Why aren't you more upset about this? How can you be so calm?"

He wiped his hand across his mouth. "Do I look calm?" He looked away from me a moment. "I guess it's because I've just about decided that Stephen's not trying to kill us."

Involuntarily I glanced at my shattered windshield. "How do you figure that?" I asked.

"Remember when Stephen was doing all that target practice out at the cabin?"

I nodded. I remembered it very well. The one time I had tried to fire Stephen's gun, instead of hitting the bull's-eye, I had hit a tree ten feet away.

"Stephen's got dead aim," Penn said. "You know that."

I was jolted by the sudden memory of Stephen laying bullet after bullet squarely on the bull's-eye. It was true. Stephen had a good eye and steady aim.

"This time he had a rifle," said Penn, "which is more accurate, and he had a tripod, but still he hit the passenger side of the windshield. What do you think about that?"

"The clap of thunder threw him off?"

"What I think is that he may have been aiming at the side of the car you weren't sitting on."

"But what about the fire at the cabin?" I asked.

"I think he meant for us to get away that time, too."

"We almost didn't, Penn!"

"I bet he didn't realize that the smoke could kill us. A lot of people don't know that. He was thinking about the fire—only the fire—and you'll notice the bedroom never did burn. Dad was able to get some of our things out of there. I don't think Stephen wanted to kill us—I think he wanted to scare the heck out of us."

"Well, gee, that makes me feel a whole lot better."

Penn smiled. "You're laughing at me. Okay, maybe I'm wrong, but I don't know—it makes me feel better somehow."

We sat in silence for a while. Then I said, delicately, "What would be the point in scaring us, Penn? If he's not trying to kill us, what's he trying to do?"

"Make us run."

I stared at him uncomprehendingly.

"Remember what I was saying at lunch? That we should just pick up and leave town? *That's what he wants!* The police would figure I had killed Laurie, and then Stephen could relax."

It was possible that Penn's theory was right. I didn't believe it, but it was possible. Certain things about it made sense. The only thing was—I wasn't sure I wanted to bet my life on it.

"He's hitting at the things that I care about," Penn said. "The cabin. And now you. He's figuring I'll panic."

"But even if you're right and he's only trying to make us run, don't you see that when we don't run, he may figure he *has* to kill us?"

Penn's eyes met mine. "I guess that's a chance we're going to have to take."

"What are you getting at?" I asked him.

Rain was coming down steadily now. Penn's hair was plastered to his forehead, and his shirt was sticking to him, but he scarcely noticed. "You're getting wet!" I cried when he didn't answer at once. "Get in the car!" I threw open the back door.

He wiped his forearm across his face clumsily and got in. He rested his hand next to my shoulder and bent forward in the seat so that he was close to my ear. He spoke very softly. "I read that story about that radical who gave herself up, Joanna. It was creepy. All these years she's been moving around the country, changing her name over and over—she's got a kid! She's going to go to prison and leave her kid!"

"She shouldn't have given herself up," I said.

"What kind of a life is that? Moving around all the time, afraid to get a good job, afraid every time you see a cop, afraid to talk about anything that ever happened to you because something you say might give you away." I noticed that the side windows of the car had fogged over. "It'd be like being a zombie, a living death," Penn said. He licked his lips. "Her folks didn't even know she was still alive until she gave herself up the other day."

I stared ahead at the fractured windshield, listening to the rain drum on the metal roof.

"We can't run," said Penn bleakly. "There's no way out."

Policemen were walking around outside still, I knew. For now we were safe from Stephen, I thought. But only for now.

When I first met Penn, my world seemed like a dazzling expanse of light and color, and I half suspected we were both immortal. It seemed odd how our lives had shrunk suddenly. Now we sat shivering, grateful even for this small safe place out of the rain.

Slowly I became conscious of a tapping on the window. A dark-coated figure was standing outside. I rolled down the window.

Captain Kronkie's thin features were tightly framed by the shining black hood of a raincoat that buttoned closely over his chin. A drop of water glistened on his beaked nose. "Good afternoon," he said. "We'll take care of your car for you, Miss Rigsby. Leave the keys in it. We'd like to ask you a few questions. You can ride downtown with me."

I got out and stood up under the large black umbrella he held for me. Rain seeped into my shoes. Penn threw open the back door, but Captain Kronkie stopped him by holding up a hand. "That's all right, Parrish. You stay here. You don't have to come."

"I'd like to come along," insisted Penn.

"You were following Miss Rigsby in your car when the incident occurred, weren't you?" inquired Captain Kronkie.

"That's right. I—" Penn began.

"So you couldn't have fired the shot and you couldn't have seen anything. You're not involved in this at all. I'll talk to the young lady alone, if you don't mind."

Penn stood in the rain watching as I climbed into the back of the police car. Another policeman was in the car, a sad-faced man with eyebrows that slanted down and deep lines running from his nostrils to the corners of his mouth. When I opened the door and got in, he turned his collar up. It pressed into the reddish flesh at the back of his bulging neck. "We need this rain," he said. "It's been right dry lately."

A crisscross of thin metal bars separated the front seats from the back, making the backseat a cage. My jeans felt clammy. I smoothed the material over my thighs.

I didn't say much on the drive to the police station. Captain Kronkie and the other officer discussed the weather at length. Not as hot as last year. The tobacco crop behind schedule. It's not the heat; it's the humidity, they agreed. I scarcely listened. I was concentrating on what I would say once the police started asking serious questions. Stephen, Penn, and even Tessa had been questioned by the police after Laurie's death, but somehow I hadn't thought it would happen to me. "You're a civilian," Tessa had said once. I had continued to think of myself as an innocent bystander, even as I was helping Penn destroy evidence. Since I hadn't expected to be brought in to the police station, I hadn't given much thought to what story I would give them. The bullet through my windshield had changed that. Now I had to come up with something convincing. I knew I would feel like a fool, insisting that I had no idea why anyone would shoot at me, but as far as I could see, that would have to be my story, even though my brain was shrieking *Stephen! Arrest Stephen!*

Captain Kronkie glanced up at his rearview mirror. "The boy is following us," he commented. "He hasn't learned how to take no for an answer."

I turned around and looked through the back window at the blurred dab of red that meant Penn's car was behind us. It was comforting to know he was there, even though I knew he couldn't help me.

I thought of the way the police had covered up the tripod marks, and an insane hope sprang up in me that they would crack the case and catch Stephen without our help. If only they could prove Stephen had shot at me! If they could do that, then no one would believe him if he claimed Penn had been the one to push Laurie over the cliff.

Water streamed down the window of the police car. Staring out the window, I felt despair creep into my heart. A few dents in the dirt and some cigarette stubs didn't amount to much in the way of evidence. The cigarettes would turn out to be a common brand; the rifle would conveniently disappear. Stephen was smart—I couldn't believe that they would catch him.

When we arrived at the station, Captain Kronkie ushered me into his office. A middle-aged woman whose straight dark hair was combed with gray came in and sat in a chair beside the desk. She was wearing black-rimmed glasses, the sort that have half-moon-shaped lenses so she could easily look over them. She peered over them at me and then turned the page of her steno pad. Captain Kronkie sat behind the desk and folded his hands, and I saw the dull golden gleam of a wedding band on his ring finger.

"Will you tell us exactly what happened?" he asked. "Mrs. Perry will take down everything you say and type it up for you to sign." He smiled. "It's called making a statement."

I laced my fingers and let my hands fall to my lap to stop them from shaking. Speaking slowly and carefully, I gave my account. I had been slowing down, I explained, when the thunder sounded and my windshield shattered. It wasn't hard to talk about it, and I was vaguely pleased with how well I was handling it.

I felt detached from the event, as if it had happened to someone else or I had seen it in a movie. When I had finished, Captain Kronkie nodded to the stenographer. She got up and exited, leaving the door propped open. I made a motion to get up, too, but Captain Kronkie waved me back to my seat.

"Just a few more questions, Miss Rigsby," he said smoothly. "Tell me, were you driving the route you usually take when you drive home from school?"

"I guess so," I said. Although Penn and I had vowed we were going to change the routes we used, it was not easy to change everyday habits. I had been upset when I got in my car, and without thinking, I had turned the car the same way as usual.

"So anyone who wanted to shoot you would be pretty sure you would drive that way after school," he suggested.

"I suppose so. But Mr. Dockerty thinks it might have been somebody gunning for him," I said hopefully. "That clap of thunder probably ruined the gunman's aim, and that's why he hit my car by mistake."

Captain Kronkie looked up at me. "You can thank that thunderstorm for your life," he said.

I hugged myself, suddenly cold. "Unless he was aiming at Mr. Dockerty," I insisted.

"If he were aiming at Mr. Dockerty, he would have lined up his gun facing the other lane of traffic, don't you think? It would be easier to get a bead on the driver through the windshield than through his back window." He smiled. "Now why would anybody want to kill you, Miss Rigsby?"

"I don't know." There was a long uncomfortable silence until finally I added, "There's a lot of mindless violence these days."

"Yes, there is." He shuffled some papers. "Particularly when you and your friends are around."

"I don't see why you say that," I said, annoyed. "I'm not the one who was doing the shooting. You ought to be trying to find out who shot at me instead of giving me a hard time."

"Don't tell me how to do my job, Miss Rigsby," he said. "The people at the school tell me you're a very smart girl, and I'll bet you know what being an accessory to a crime means. Did you know that women usually get stiffer prison sentences than men do for the same offense? That's because juries figure they should've known better." He snapped his ballpoint pen open with his thumb. He regarded me through half-closed eyes. "I think you should have known better than to get mixed up with this crowd."

"What do my friends have to do with it?" I protested. "And when are you going to start working on finding out who shot at me?" Suddenly I remembered my claim that he was shooting at Mr. Dockerty. "Or Mr. Dockerty," I finished lamely.

"I have my ideas about that," he said. "But I don't think I'm going to get very far in this case without your help."

"How could I help?" I cried. "I don't know who fired the gun. I have no idea."

"Would you agree to take a lie detector test?" he suggested.

My heart fluttered wildly. "No. I don't believe in those things. They aren't accurate. I won't take one."

He leaned back in his chair. "I didn't think you would. I'll tell you something—you'd better try telling the truth. The next time this guy comes gunning for you, you may not be so lucky."

I'm not sure how I got out of the building. My legs seemed unsteady, and when I stepped into the bright light, I winced. I felt so vulnerable once I was out in the open that it took all my determination to keep from throwing myself to the ground. I wanted to crawl to Penn's car on my belly. It would have felt safer.

The sidewalks and pavement were shiny with rain, but the downpour had stopped. Penn was waiting in the Corvette. I got in quickly. Even so close to the police station, I was frightened, knowing that Stephen was still out there somewhere with his rifle. "They aren't even trying to catch him, Penn," I said bleakly. "What are we going to do?"

Penn took a deep breath and gunned the engine.

"I don't know what we do next," said Penn as we sped away. "I hope we think of something. Soon."

> . . . *Diary, I wonder if I should have encouraged Penn to make a run for it. I'm not sure I'm thinking straight anymore. What if Stephen finds out that the police have had us in for questioning again? He's got to be worried that we're going to crack and spill out the truth. That's why Penn's theory doesn't make sense. Stephen would be taking a big chance if he was only trying to scare us. The more scared we are, the more likely we are to blurt out something damaging to the police.*
>
> *He didn't even try to make this last at-*

tempt look like an accident. He must be desperate. If his idea was to make us run, pretty soon he'll know that it didn't work. My blood runs cold when I think of that bullet they pulled out of my seat cushion.

Ten

My father buttered his breakfast muffin. He looked up suddenly from the spreadsheet he was going over before work. "A bullet hit the windshield?" He stared at me incredulously. "You're kidding me."

"There's a lot of random violence these days," I said. "I read about it all the time."

"Not in Barton City. Or at least not very often. Where did this happen?"

"Right in front of the school."

"Right in front of the school?" he repeated. "Have they caught anybody yet? Do they have any leads? Was some kid running around firing at everything in sight, or what?"

I shook my head. "It could have been an accident. A hunter maybe," I said.

"That doesn't make any sense," my father said. "There's nothing to hunt out there by the school. It's a quiet neighborhood with mailboxes, sprinklers, and swimming pools. Nobody's going to stalk deer through somebody else's begonias." Leaving his buttered muffin congealing on the plate, he stepped out of the kitchen, and I hoped the interrogation was over. But a minute later he reappeared with a city-county map and spread it out on the kitchen table. "Look," he said, smoothing the creases out of the map. "To the south of the school are the new subdivisions— Sherwood Forest, Southridge Village, High Meadows—and to the north, from the school to Sunset Avenue, are old neighborhoods with the houses close together, lots of retired people. There's no hunting land, not even farmland, for two miles in any direction, and if an ordinary rifle bullet can go more than a mile, it's news to me."

"It could be a freak accident," I said. "A gun could have fired when somebody was loading it onto his truck, maybe."

He refolded the map carefully, accordion style, then looked at me closely. "Are you giving me the whole story, Joanna?"

"What do you mean?" I squeaked.

"I mean, you haven't gotten involved in

drugs, have you?" He hesitated. "Not that I really think you have, but I hear things at work about what kids get into these days."

I shook my head. He should get together with Penn's dad, I thought. It had begun to strike me as comical the way that neither of them could seem to imagine anything that might go wrong except drugs. "Accidents do happen," I insisted stubbornly.

"Yeah." He frowned. "But you're starting to look accident-prone. I know I'm busy and not around much, maybe. Do you need to talk to somebody? They have these therapist people. I could get somebody at work to recommend one."

It occurred to me that my father thought maybe I was making up these stories of my close escapes from death in order to get attention. That must be why he was talking about therapists. I turned around, twisted the tap on, and washed my hands. "No, I'm fine," I said. I was relieved that my voice sounded reasonably steady. "The car will be out of the shop day after tomorrow. They told me insurance will cover it. It's no big deal," I said, turning to face him.

He glanced at his watch. "I gotta go. Well, if you change your mind, let me know." He hastily stuffed the rest of the muffin in his mouth and wiped his buttery fingers on a paper napkin.

While I was stuffing my books into my book bag, I heard him gargling at the back of the house. He would be out of the house in five minutes and would probably have his secretary come up with the names of three therapists suitable for daughters who were suffering from the delusion that people were shooting at them. My father might not be insightful, but he was efficient.

A moment later I heard Penn's car drive up, and went outside. He had shown up to drive me to school, since I was without my car.

"How did your father take the news?" he asked.

I smiled grimly. "I think he's decided I'm making it up to get attention."

Penn raised his eyebrows. "He thinks you smashed your own windshield just so he'll come home for dinner more often? That's crazy."

"I know, but he's not crazy. He's not even stupid. It's that he's not paying attention. How did your father take it?"

"I haven't told him yet. If my name was going to show up in the newspaper story, then I'd have to tell him. I wouldn't have any choice, because everybody at the hospital would be talking about it nonstop." Penn grinned. "But you heard Captain Kronkie. I'm not involved."

"My name will be in the newspaper story, though, and your dad is bound to recognize that."

"You think my dad reads the paper?" Penn raised his eyebrows. "Wrong! The only way he's going to find out about this is if somebody at the hospital tells him. And they won't because they won't recognize your name," he said triumphantly. "So I didn't tell him anything. All I said was that the drug clinic called and I had to reschedule the visit."

"Did he believe you?"

"Nah. You know we drug addicts lie, cheat, and steal," Penn said. "Right now he's trying to rebuild the communication between us. He must have read a pamphlet about how to do it or something. It's pretty grim. Last night he staggers in at ten, and he's so tired he's gray in the face, you know? And he says in this phony way, 'Well, now, why don't you and I do something together?'"

I grinned.

"So—get this—we end up sitting cross-legged on the floor, newspaper spread all over, polishing our shoes! Have you ever heard of anything so weird?" Penn gazed absently at the road ahead. "He talked about his work, what else? It's all he knows about. But the funny thing is he ended up saying something really interesting."

"About his work?" I was puzzled. I had never heard Penn admit that anything about his father's work interested him.

"It turns out Mrs. Landen is a patient of his," Penn said.

I was puzzled. Mrs. Landen?

"Oh, I forgot. You wouldn't know her," he said. "She was an English teacher back when we were in the ninth grade, but then she retired."

Road construction was going on just ahead of us, and we had to slow down. I found myself cringing instinctively, as if I expected a rifle shot through the windshield every time we slowed down. Orange cones blocked off the turn lane, and a truck was stopped at the end of them, its crane propped up and silhouetted black against the sky.

"Can't we speed up a little?" I asked.

Penn grinned. "What happened to 'Slow down, Penn'? That's what you usually say."

"I don't know." I took a deep breath. Power lines crisscrossed the sky over us like a vast metal spiderweb. I felt as if we were caught, and I was having trouble concentrating on what Penn was saying.

"Are you okay, Joanna?" He gave me a worried look.

"I can't help it," I said unsteadily. "I don't have your steady nerves. I'm not used to crawling out of burning houses and getting shot at. I keep looking around, wondering where Stephen could be hiding."

Penn squeezed my knee. "It's okay. Calm down. I'm taking the long way around. Didn't you notice? He'd never expect us to loop around Whittier Street." He grinned. "And when we get close to school, you can scrunch down under the dash if you want."

"Okay." He might laugh, but that sounded good to me. Let Penn take a bullet through his windshield and see how calm he'd be then, I thought.

"Did you hear anything I said a minute ago?" he asked.

"Old English teacher. Retired," I repeated automatically.

"Right. Mrs. Landen's her name. She's been in the hospital." He shot me a quick glance. "And all her newspapers piled up while she was gone. She only started sorting through them yesterday, and that's when she saw the story about Stephen being a National Merit Scholar. It got her so upset, she started having heart palpitations. So she called Dad's office to ask if maybe she should go back in the hospital. She's gotten hard of hearing, so talking to her over the phone is kind of ridiculous. Dad said he could hear Barbara, that's his nurse, yelling, 'You'd better come in!' all the way into his examining room."

"I don't get it. Why was she so upset about the newspaper story?"

"Mrs. Landen was the teacher who gave Stephen the C."

"Oh."

"Remember how it said in the newspaper that Stephen was second in his class? She knew there was no way he could be second in the class, because of that C. Of course, she never did like him."

Maybe the old lady was a good judge of character, I thought.

"Dad asked me if I knew anything about the grade Mrs. Landen gave Stephen," Penn went on. "He wondered if she remembered wrong. He figured maybe she was confused. She's had bypass surgery, and sometimes that has bad side effects."

"What did you say?"

"I said no, I didn't know anything about it. I figured why should I know about some grade

Stephen got when we were in the ninth grade? It was years ago. Of course, I was about to pass out, I was so nervous the whole time I was saying it." He shook his head. "That stupid C she gave him. Who could have figured it would lead to this? Laurie and Casey are dead, and you and I are wondering if we're going to live to graduate."

I could feel gears clicking in my mind. "Penn," I cried suddenly, "maybe this is a way out! Do you think Mrs. Landen might call Mr. Hansen and complain about Stephen's average being wrong?"

Penn shrugged. "I don't know."

"But if she did—think of it! The whole story might come out and Stephen could end up in jail!"

"You're not thinking straight. Nobody's going to put Stephen in jail because somehow his grade point average got messed up."

Penn was right, I realized with a sudden sick feeling. Even if Mrs. Landen lodged a formal complaint about the grade and the necessary correction was made, still nothing linked Stephen to the two murders except Penn, Tessa, and me—the eyewitnesses. "Then Mrs. Landen's finding out about the grade change doesn't mean a thing," I said.

"I'm not so sure of that," said Penn slowly.

"What do you mean?"

"How long do you think that old lady is going to live if she tries to take that National Merit Scholarship away from Stephen?"

I sucked in my breath. "You really think he might try to kill her?"

"I don't know." Penn shrugged. "I don't know if she's even going to complain. If she does, I don't know if Stephen would even care. He's going to Rutgers, not Princeton the way he thought, remember. Rutgers is a lot cheaper school. He might not need the scholarship as much."

"But, Penn—he'd have to worry that the whole story would come out!"

"It probably wouldn't, though."

"It's not like he's cool about it," I argued.

"No." Penn turned onto the thoroughfare. "I guess you'd have to say he's panicking."

I sagged back against the seat. "She won't call and complain," I said listlessly. "Nothing is going to happen except that Stephen is going to keep trying to kill us until finally he does it."

"Hey, get a grip, Joanna!" Penn smiled as he let his cupped fingers slide down my cheek. "We aren't dead yet."

The student lot was full of tightly packed cars and kids getting out and calling to their friends. Car tape players blared.

Only the puddles underfoot remained of yesterday's thunderstorm. This morning the sky was rinsed clear, and light sparkled on the hoods and windshields of the cars. Stephen would never try anything here, I told myself as I got out of the car. Not with all these people around. But I found myself nervously checking around me just the same.

"Joanna!"

Instinctively I ducked. My heart pounding, I cowered beside Penn's car. Penn gave me a hand and pulled me up. "Be cool. It's only Nikki," he said in a warning voice.

"Oh, I'm so sorry!" cried Nikki, running over to me. "I didn't mean to scare you."

I flecked the gravel off my knees. "I guess I'm a little jumpy," I admitted.

"I don't blame you, you poor thing." Nikki's face was screwed up into an expression of sympathy. "Being shot at like that! I'm surprised you even made it to school today. I mean, you could have been killed!"

I smiled weakly. "Oh, the bullet missed me by a good thirty inches."

Nikki shuddered. "I didn't see it happen"—
her tone was distinctly regretful—"but Mandy
Hargrove called me after I got in from school
and told me all about it. Is it true the police
think he was actually trying to shoot Mr.
Dockerty?"

My gaze flicked toward Penn. "I'm not sure."

"Well, Dockerty really is a hard grader," Nikki
said.

"I don't think that's any reason to blow the
guy away," put in Penn.

"Oh, no!" cried Nikki. "I didn't mean that."
Her cheeks were pink with excitement. "But you
know there are a lot of nuts running around. You
never can tell what some people will do. Did you
see the thing in the paper about the boy who
went berserk at some school in California?
Mandy said she thought the senior class gift
ought to be a metal detector."

"I like it," said Penn. "Simple, practical."

"It may go over our budget, though," said
Nikki regretfully. "I read somewhere that the really good ones cost a lot, and you know, when
you think about it, the best metal detector in the
world wouldn't have stopped what happened to
Joanna, or what happened to Casey, either, for
that matter."

Nikki might have said more, but she saw
Stephen and Tessa approaching. She and Tessa
were old enemies. "Well, see ya," she said with
an uneasy smile. "Take it easy for a while.
Something like that's a real shock to your nervous system."

Tell me about it, I thought, pressing my hand
to my belly.

Stephen peeled off his black gloves as he approached, and I couldn't take my eyes off his
hands, pale with long fingers. I remembered how
he had been wearing those black gloves the night
Casey was shot. I had seen his black-gloved fingers around the butt of the pistol and had seen it
leap in his hand when it fired. I told myself it was
better to have him in plain sight instead of lurk-
ing behind a bush somewhere with a rifle. He
couldn't do anything to me in the parking lot in
full view of half the school.

"You look so pale!" Tessa laid a hand on my
shoulder and peered into my eyes with earnest
sympathy. "I heard what happened!" she said.
"It's beyond everything. After all we've been
through, now you have to dodge a bullet meant
for Dockerty."

Stephen's eyes were luminous and his cheeks
were flushed, as if he were a child just awakened

from a nap. His hair was wild, one dark strand falling over an eyebrow. "You wouldn't think anybody hated Dockerty that much, would you?" he said sweetly.

"Who told you they were after Dockerty?" asked Penn quietly.

"Oh, it's all over the school!" cried Tessa. "Two people told me before I even got my helmet off. Besides, what else could it be? Joanna hasn't even been here long enough to make any enemies."

"It could be a homicidal maniac, I guess," said Penn. His voice was steady. "They say somebody can look perfectly normal and you can know them for years and then, pow, they blow up. That's when you realize there are all kinds of creepy, crawly things going on inside them."

Stephen flushed angrily. I tugged at Penn's arm. I was afraid he was going to goad Stephen too far.

"I honestly don't think there is anybody like that at Barton High," said Tessa. "Look around you! Everybody even *looks* boring! I suppose it could have been accidental. Remember when they arrested that kid out at the county high school? He was carrying a gun in his book bag and it went off by accident. Luckily nobody was hurt."

"This wasn't an accident," said Penn. "The cops found tripod marks." With a quick glance at Stephen, he added, "And cigarette butts."

"Isn't there DNA in saliva? You'd think they could trace him that way," said Tessa.

"Maybe they will," said Penn.

Stephen unconsciously squeezed his nicotine-stained middle finger, his eyes on Penn. "Was it a common brand or what?" he asked.

"I don't know," said Penn. "The cops won't tell me anything."

When the four of us parted at the administration building, Tessa gave me a quick hug and smiled.

"I halfway feel like telling Tessa," I said bitterly as we walked away from them. "That dumb, innocent pose of hers is beginning to get to me."

"She wouldn't believe you," said Penn. He was walking with long strides, and I had to run to keep up. "If she doesn't see what's going on now, it's because she doesn't want to."

"Or else she's in with him," I said.

"I don't believe that," Penn said flatly.

I was angry at her as if she had been in on it. If we had been sure we could count on Tessa, we might be able to risk going to the police. But I knew we couldn't depend on her. If she had to choose between us and Stephen, there wasn't any doubt in my mind what she'd do.

"I have to go by my locker," said Penn grimly. "Don't turn your back on Stephen while I'm gone, okay?"

I think it was an instinct to take cover that made me duck into the rest room a moment later. It was one place Stephen wouldn't follow me. The small frosted-glass windows were high overhead. Any bullet that came flying through them would miss me. I combed my hair, parted my lips, and examined my teeth carefully in the mirror. Knowing that there was a foot-thick cement-block wall between me and the outside walkway, I breathed easier. I wished I could stay in the bathroom forever. I turned to leave, and to my astonishment the door flew open and I ran smack into Tessa.

"Excuse me," she said in a muffled voice.

The class bell rang, but neither of us made a move to leave. We were alone with the dank smell of the place. Tessa's face was as pale as marble. Only the curve of her lips and the delicate scroll of her ears showed the pink flush of life. She wiped a tear from her eye. Her black lashes stuck together in points, making a starry fringe to the dark eyes swimming with tears.

"Are you okay?" I asked, touching her arm.

"F-fine," she said. She and Stephen both had the habit of stuttering when they were rattled. "You probably think I'm pretty stupid," she choked. "Here, you're the one who got shot at and I'm the one who's bawling."

"I don't think it's stupid at all," I said. "What's the matter?"

"I'm worried about Stephen," she said tremulously. She took a long shuddering breath. "He's not eating, and when I hug him, I can feel his bones."

"His clothes are so loose," I said. "I hadn't noticed." Not to mention that I had my mind on more pressing things, such as staying alive.

I was startled when Tessa bent over, but she was only checking to make sure no one was in the stalls. She lowered her voice almost to a whisper. "I think he blames himself for what happened to Casey," she said. "He's haunted by it. It was bad enough after Laurie, but now, since Casey—he can't forgive himself."

"You don't think he's just afraid of getting caught?" I suggested.

Tessa's eyes flashed. "What do you mean by that! You know it was an accident."

"Listen to me, Tessa," I cried. "Maybe—just maybe—it wasn't an accident."

Tessa closed her eyes tight and covered her ears with her hands. "Stop it!" she cried. "I'm not going to listen to you!"

Furious, I pulled her hands away from her ears. "Hasn't it hit you that he must have been the one who shot at me yesterday?"

She stared at me incredulously. "You are going out of your mind!"

"He smokes like a chimney, and there were three cigarette butts right where the gunman stood," I insisted. "What's the logical conclusion?"

Tessa pulled away and regarded me furiously. "I am going to forget you ever said that," she spat. "You don't know Stephen as well as I do. In fact, you don't even know Penn as well as I do. That's why you're saying these things. I really think you must be temporarily deranged by the fright you had yesterday. That's the only explanation." She groped for the door.

"But what if I'm right? What if Stephen is a murderer?" I insisted.

She wheeled around furiously to face me. "Say whatever you want to me, Joanna, but if you say one word to anyone else—if you harm one hair on Stephen's head—I'll make sure you regret it as long as you live."

Her ominous tone chilled me. I watched the

door swing shut behind her with a sick feeling.
Penn had warned me she wouldn't believe me. I
wished I had listened to him.

Dear Diary,
    What have I done? I've made an enemy
of Tessa. I wish I hadn't sprung it on her the
way I did. Maybe if I had been more tactful
. . . No! Who am I kidding? Nothing I could
have said would have made any difference.
Stephen and Tessa are like halves of a
whole. They share everything—they breathe
in harmony. Tessa helped hide Laurie's body,
and even typed the so-called suicide note
Casey left. They didn't share in the murders,
but somehow she's persuaded herself that
both deaths were accidents.
    One thing's for sure—this is the end of
the pretending. Tessa's bound to tell Stephen
what I said. He knows what I think—he
read my diary, after all. But now everything's out in the open. We won't be eating
lunch together or standing around in the
parking lot smiling at each other.

Eleven

. . . How am I going to tell Penn what I've done? He warned me that Tessa wouldn't believe me.

I was conscious of Bobby's gaze when I slunk into homeroom late. Trying to be inconspicuous, I sat down at once behind Bobby. He was slouched behind his desk. His hair had been shaved above the ear, exposing a white strip of bare skin. The wild tufts of hair on top of his head stood out. It was the sort of haircut cannibals might have used to terrify their enemies. A knee with a scab on it poked out of his ripped jeans.

The bell for first period rang. "What gives?" Bobby asked. "Somebody told me you got shot at yesterday." He stood up suddenly, blocking my way.

The raucous noises of the hallway filtered through the doorway. "Oh, it was Mr. Dockerty they were shooting at." I managed a weak smile. "Not me."

"Nah! Dockerty's been around here twenty years, and nobody's taken a shot at him yet. You're the one. What I can't figure out is why." His brow was furrowed with the unaccustomed effort of thought.

"I have to go, Bobby," I said. "I'm going to be late to class."

His eyes narrowed in suspicion. "I'll come along."

I couldn't stop him. "I don't know what you want me to say, Bobby," I said. I felt as if I were being followed by an embarrassingly large stray dog. "It's not like I know who shot at me. I was driving along in front of the school minding my own business, and suddenly the windshield shattered into a million pieces. I really think they were after Mr. Dockerty."

"Don't give me that. What's your first-period class?"

"English." For an awful moment I was afraid he planned to sit next to me in English and watch me the entire hour with those suspicious bloodshot eyes. Bobby didn't operate according to the normal rules.

Suddenly we ran headlong into Tessa.

"Whoa," said Bobby, steadying me with both hands.

Tessa looked full into my face, her eyes blazing; then she stalked off without saying a word.

"What's eating her?" asked Bobby, staring after her.

"I guess she's having a bad day." I lengthened my stride. The close-packed crowd in the hallways parted to make way for us. No one wanted to risk bumping into Bobby, not since a few months ago when he pitched a boy over the railing.

"Something's going on," said Bobby suspiciously. "And I'm gonna find out what it is."

His words sent a chill up my spine.

"Does Tessa know how to shoot a rifle?" he asked suddenly.

"How should I know?" I cried. The idea of Bobby playing detective might have struck me as comical in better days. But right now I wasn't laughing.

"Maybe I'll have a little talk with Tessa, ask her some questions," he said.

"No!" I cried. "Don't do that!"

"What's the matter? Afraid of what she's going to say?"

A truthful answer would have been yes. It would take only one word from Tessa to make Bobby berserk, and I didn't want to be around when that happened.

When we got to my class, I turned around to confront him. "Give me a break," I pleaded. "I'm still upset about being shot at, and you're not helping me any. Tessa and I had a fight, that's all. It's nothing. None of your business."

"A fight? What about?" He watched me closely.

"It was stupid, really. I don't want to talk about it."

"Why not? What's the big secret?"

"Oh, Bobby! Go away!" I cried.

He laughed, and after a minute's hesitation he slouched off.

When I went in the classroom, a girl I had met at one of Bobby's parties leaned her elbow on her desk and smiled at me. A cascade of thin black braids fell over the shoulder that was bared by her sleeveless tank top. Her gold nose stud gleamed discreetly. "I saw Bobby chasing you," she said. "You ditching Penn now or what?"

I closed my eyes and took a deep breath. "Don't be stupid."

"Well, keep your hair on," she said. "I was just asking."

I felt like one of those jugglers who keeps throwing plates up in the air until finally they are coming so fast that all at once they come crashing down. Penn was right, I thought. Everyone was closing in. The police. Stephen. Tessa. And now Bobby. I shut my eyes and had the sensation that the room was whirling dizzily around me.

At lunch I caught Penn outside the cafeteria before he went in. "Wait!" I said, pulling him aside. "Don't go in. I've got to tell you something."

He glanced around uneasily. "I'm kind of trying to stay where there's no open line of fire," he said. "Let's go inside."

I pulled him close and lowered my voice. "Penn, I told Tessa."

He stared at me blankly. "You what?"

"I don't know—it just happened," I said miserably. "I told her. And now she's really mad."

"Damn!"

"She didn't believe me. No matter what I said, she wouldn't have believed me."

"What did you expect?"

"I had to try."

Penn's mouth was steady, but the darkness in

his eyes was a clue to the turbulence inside him. "It doesn't make any difference," he said at last.

"She's really mad," I went on unhappily. "She cut me dead in the hall. Bobby thought she was acting so weird, he asked me what was going on."

"Where does Bobby fit in?" asked Penn.

"He's never given up trying to find out who killed Laurie, you know that. And he doesn't trust any of us. I feel like he's watching me all the time. He even said he might ask Tessa some questions!"

Penn smiled crookedly. "Maybe we should leave town after all." He shrugged. "Well, let's get something to eat. No point in starving."

"You mean go into the cafeteria?" I hung back.

"Safest place in the world," he said promptly. "Tessa never could stand cafeteria food, and Stephen's given up eating."

So he, too, had noticed that Stephen had lost weight.

Reluctantly I trailed inside. The acrid smell of burnt grease stung my nostrils. "Smells like hamburgers and french fries," said Penn. "Could be worse."

As we joined the line, I was conscious of furtive, curious looks. A couple of kids near us edged away.

Sweat ran down the faces of some of the people serving, and a blue haze hung over the grill at the back. The woman who shoveled french fries on my plate said, "You the one that got shot at?"

I nodded.

"I don't know what the world's coming to," she exclaimed. "They're going to kill us all in our beds, next." One of her front teeth was gold. Shaking her white-capped head at me, she handed my plate on to the next worker, a thin, sour-faced woman wearing a hair net. Without comment, the sour-faced lady added a gray hamburger patty to a cottony bun.

Even the workers in the cafeteria line knew who we were. Our bunch must look like a human Bermuda Triangle, I realized—one disaster after another. We had become notorious. A lot of wild rumors had gone around school, like Laurie had been a sacrifice in our devil-worshiping rites, but I could laugh at that. What bothered me was the feeling that everybody was watching us to see who would die next.

Penn and I sat down at an empty table, and I glanced around at the noisy cafeteria. Plates and trays clattered; a french fry landed at my feet. "I wonder where Stephen and Tessa are?" I asked.

He shrugged. "Dunno. Telling lies to the

police? Having a picnic? Take your pick."

"What are we going to do, Penn? We can't spend the rest of our lives diving for cover."

"I don't know why not." Spots of color burned high on his cheekbones. He popped a french fry into his mouth. "It's not like we expect to live all that long."

"Penn!" I covered his hand with mine. "Stop it," I urged. "We're going to make it. We're getting out of this alive."

"I hope," he said. He glanced up at the clock by the window. I knew what he was thinking. Time might be running out.

As I went through the motions of going to classes that afternoon, I was uncomfortably aware of how we must look to Captain Kronkie. Penn with his sleek blond hair, his Corvette, and his ready answers must look too smooth to believe. Stephen and Tessa and I weren't much better—good students but peculiar. There wasn't a member of student government or the tennis team among us. Instead of competing in wholesome American sports, we had the habit of going off by ourselves to an isolated cabin in the woods. Now one by one and for no apparent reason, we were dying violent deaths.

Captain Kronkie knew we were lying to him. He couldn't prove it, but he knew it, all right. No wonder he was in no hurry to help us out.

I wondered if it would be possible for Penn and me to turn state's evidence. Captain Kronkie didn't like us, but maybe we wouldn't have to deal with him. Maybe we could go straight to the district attorney. Was there any chance he would let us off completely for testifying against Stephen and Tessa? I tried to remember everything I had read in the newspaper about criminals who testified for the prosecution, but I was having a hard time thinking. My head ached and I was tired.

Now that I was seriously considering going to the police, I understood better what had held Penn back. It was tough dodging fire and bullets, but at least every day there was a chance we might escape. Once we gave ourselves up to the police, there was no escape. Captain Kronkie would take us into custody and the engine of the law would grind us to bits. I could imagine Penn and me in handcuffs, our faces whitened by newspaper flashbulbs. Arrested. Jailed. Sitting alone in cells with thin, stained mattresses and brown-streaked plumbing.

Twelve

When I got to physics class that afternoon, I was startled to see that the blinds in the classroom had been pulled shut and the overhead lights had been turned on. Since Dockerty was a fresh-air fiend who normally never closed the windows, it didn't take a genius to figure out what was going on. He was afraid somebody might shoot at him from the other wing. The wall of windows in the classroom must have looked to him like an open invitation to a sniper.

"Miss Rigsby?" he said. I snapped to attention at my name.

"Would you take these forms to the office for me?" He shook the papers. "They sent me the wrong ones again."

Mechanically I rose, took the papers, and headed out the door. As I walked through Eastman's deserted passageway, I could hear the stealthy whisper of my shoe soles on the cement. Over the railing lay the broad plot of lawn between the wing and the cafeteria building. There, sunlight lay in pools and dandelion puffs floated above the grass on invisible stems. Leaving the wing, I went past the crossed sidewalks with their litter of gum wrappings and crumbled notebook paper. Beside the front door of the administration building, a pair of pink azaleas clashed fiercely with the orange of the brick.

When I swung the door open, to my astonishment, Tessa stood behind the counter sorting through the mail. Gulping, I laid the forms down on the counter, but she gave no sign that she had seen me.

"Mr. Dockerty says the office gave him the wrong forms," I said.

She regarded me coolly for a long second and then picked up the forms and turned away. "Mrs. Parker, are these the wrong forms?" She took them over to an older woman sitting in front of a computer screen, her mouth gaping in intense concentration.

I glanced down. The envelope that was faceup before me was of thick creamy paper and was addressed in spidery handwriting. It looked like a personal letter, completely unlike the other mail. I twisted my neck to get a better look and was able to read the return address:

Martha Landen
302 Greenacre Lane

Mrs. Landen had written the school! For a moment I was afraid to breathe.

Tessa returned at once with a stack of forms. "Take him these," she said shortly.

I took the forms and turned away, but out of the corner of my eye I saw Tessa pick up the cream-colored envelope. With a quick sideways glance to make sure no one was looking, she slipped it under the counter. Then I heard a faint metallic snap. She had put it in her pocketbook and snapped the clasp shut. Pale now, her dark eyes wide open with alarm, she stood up and returned to her task. As if nothing had happened, she contin- ued sorting mail into three wooden bins that lay on the counter.

Should I stop here and accuse her of stealing the letter? I wondered. Something in me shrank from another scene. Besides, I told my-self, what would be the point? Penn had al-ready explained that nothing Mrs. Landen could tell Mr. Hansen would tie Stephen to the murders.

I stepped outside, and the suddenly bright light stunned me momentarily. The sidewalks around the building were deserted and silent. On the steps in front of the auditorium, a boy sat holding a violin case.

I stared at the forms in my hand with disbe-lief, scarcely able to remember why I had come to the office to get them. Mr. Dockerty needed the forms, I reminded myself. I should take them to him. But first I've got to find Penn. The thought was like a siren in my brain. Our schedules didn't mesh at all, and usually when he was in one wing, I was in the other. I wasn't exactly sure of where his classes were, but he must be somewhere on the ground floor of Eastman about now, I guessed. If I walked along the passageway in Eastman just as class was letting out, there was a chance I would run into him.

But the stupid forms! If I didn't come back to class with them, Dockerty might send someone else to the office looking for me.

Quickly I walked back to Dockerty's class. The silence of the empty halls was eerie. A wasp floated at eye level for a few seconds before dropping from my sight. A sheet of paper skidded down the hallway ahead of me. I went in and quietly laid the forms on Dockerty's desk. He was putting a problem on the board and didn't even see me. Then I turned on my heel and left. The eyes of my curious classmates followed me as I tiptoed out.

Then, as if someone were chasing me, I hurried to Eastman. When I got there, breathing hard, I leaned against the brick wall of the passageway and looked out at the sunny lawn as I waited for the bell to ring. Through my thin shirt the warmth of the bricks felt good against my shoulders. Here I was safe, I told myself. Stephen would never find me, because I had cut class.

The bell rang, abruptly going off in my ear like a bomb, and at once kids began streaming out into the hallway. I pressed forward, suddenly confused, watching for Penn's ash-blond hair and his familiar walk. So many kids in jeans, sneakers, and T-shirts! I had a moment of panic that I might not recognize him even if I saw him. And then suddenly he was there. "Joanna!" he said quickly. "What's the matter?" He grabbed my arm and we hurried down the passageway together.

"Mrs. Landen has written the school," I gasped. "I saw the letter. It came in today's mail."

I could hear his quick intake of breath.

"But Mr. Hansen will never get to see it. Tessa stole it!" I whispered.

"Stole it? Why? How would she even know about it?" He looked at me, momentarily confused.

"Don't you remember? She told us about how she was going to volunteer for office duty. She's working in the office during her study hall these days."

Penn ran his fingers through his hair. "Jeez. Are you sure it was from Mrs. Landen?"

"I read the return address. It was lying on the counter. I was in the office getting some forms for Mr. Dockerty."

"Couldn't you have grabbed it?"

I flushed. "I didn't have a chance. I'd barely figured out what it was when Tessa turned around."

Penn cupped both hands over his mouth as if he were hyperventilating. I could almost see the thoughts racing behind his eyes. "I bet Mrs.

Landen wrote because she's hard of hearing," he said at last. "I remember Dad said his secretary had to scream into the phone when she was talking to her." He was thinking aloud. "She probably tries to steer clear of phones except in emergencies. Besides, if she's making a formal complaint, I guess she'd want it to be in writing."

"The envelope stood out a mile from all the other mail," I said. "It was on this thick rag stationery, cream-colored, and with a thin, wobbly handwritten address. All the rest of the envelopes looked like junk mail or bills. Mrs. Landen's letter looked completely different."

"I can't believe Tessa stole it with you right there watching her!"

"I only saw what she was doing on my way out. Besides, she probably doesn't realize that I know who Mrs. Landen is."

"She should have waited until you'd left," Penn said.

"She probably figured she'd better move fast. What if the office secretary saw it before she could get rid of it? Then she'd have been stuck."

"I wish," sighed Penn.

"I don't suppose it matters," I said.

"Tessa thinks it does," Penn pointed out. "She grabbed that letter pretty fast, didn't she?"

"That's because she's getting paranoid." I added, "They're both paranoid."

Penn glanced around. "Let's get out of here."

"You mean leave school?" I asked.

"Sure. What's the point in hanging around?"

I felt incredibly self-conscious as we walked to the parking lot. I don't know why skipping school bothered me so much. I certainly had bigger problems. I suppose it was that I didn't have much practice at breaking rules.

"I've got to think," said Penn. We drove in silence. The traffic lights swayed overhead as if they were out of control and might drop. It was a strange, oppressive day, warm with bursts of wind. At last Penn pulled up to a McDonald's. He ordered an ice-cream sundae and we took it to a table at the back.

I looked out the window at the children's playground. A plump blond toddler was going down the sliding board, her curls flying in the breeze. Overhead a brightly colored pirate figure clung to a barber-striped pole. Nearby was a life-sized shiny plastic tree.

"I wish we had gone somewhere else," I said. "This place reminds me of Casey." In fact, I had been sitting at a table in this very playground on the night Casey told me the truth about how Stephen had pushed Laurie off the cliff. He had been disgustingly drunk.

"I'm an innocent bystander," he had said, sobbing. "More sinned against than sinning."

From that moment we had all known Casey couldn't be trusted to keep his mouth shut. Looking back, I realized it was on that night that Stephen had decided to kill Casey.

Penn glanced outside. "We can't leave now. Think about something else."

I watched him scoop up nuts and soft ice cream, the sun-whitened hair on his arms, the high curve of his fair eyebrows. Usually, all I had to do was see him and I melted. But not today. My mind was flooded with the memory of Casey's nightmarish accusations and threats. That night had been the beginning of a terrifying spiral that had led to his murder.

"Stephen probably has Mrs. Landen's letter in his hot little hands by now," Penn said.

"Probably," I agreed. "Tessa must have gone to find him as soon as she could get away from the office. For all I knew, she left right after I did. She could have made up some excuse or other." I knew it would have been hard for

Tessa to stand around sorting mail as long as Mrs. Landen's letter was burning a hole in her pocketbook.

Penn frowned. "Nothing's to stop Mrs. L. from writing another letter," he said, "and if she gets Stephen's grade changed back to a C and he ends up losing that grant, it'd be a high-profile story, with him being a National Merit Scholar and all. Chances are it'd be all over the papers. I remember there was a scandal like that up in New Jersey a couple of years ago, and there was a big mess about it. He won't want that. He's got too much to hide." Penn gazed outside. The toddler had fallen down and was shrieking, her face red and contorted into a cartoon of grief. A pregnant woman leapt to her feet and ran over to help. "A story like that in the papers could spur some kind of investigation." Penn glanced at me. "Which would make him nervous as hell. The last thing he wants right now is somebody poking around trying to find out how that C happened to get changed to an A." Penn frowned. "He's going to want to do something to stop it."

"But what can he do?"

"Guess." He shot me a quick glance. "He's going to want to shut Mrs. Landen up, that's what. He's already shut up two people. Why should he hold back now?"

"Penn, we've got to warn her!" But we had no idea how or when Stephen might strike, I realized suddenly. We couldn't even be sure Mrs. Landen would believe us if we told her the truth. "What am I saying? It's hopeless," I cried. "It's not like we can post armed guards on her for the rest of her life. We can't even protect ourselves!"

"I don't think it's as bad as that," said Penn. He stirred the ice cream with his white plastic spoon. "Stephen's probably going to figure he's got about a week."

I wasn't following him. "Why only a week?"

"Because after a week, maybe two, Mrs. L. is going to start to wonder why she hasn't heard from Mr. Hansen. Then she'll write another letter or call or get somebody to call for her."

"You really think Stephen's going to try to kill Mrs. Landen?"

"I'd be willing to bet on it." His gray eyes were cold. "Think about it. The sooner he kills her, the better for him. She might try to call Mr. Hansen tomorrow. She might talk to somebody. She's already talked to my dad."

"But what can we do to stop him?" I cried.

"We'll think of something."

"I know what!" I cried. "We could make an anonymous phone call to the police and warn them that somebody's going to try to kill her!"

"All they'd do is try to keep an eye on her house. I don't think a patrol car driving by her house every night is going to be much help."

My head was whirling. Stephen had the letter! Right at this very minute he might be planning to kill Mrs. Landen! But we went on attending classes and eating ice cream as if nothing were wrong. It was crazy. It couldn't be true!

I picked up my spoon, but then I saw that Penn had finished off the entire sundae. Only a single nut crumb lay in the bottom of the sticky plastic dish. I smiled weakly. "Maybe I'll get a package of cookies," I said.

"The police are no good," said Penn suddenly. "We've got to come up with something else." He got up from the table. "I've got an idea. Let me check it out and I'll give you a call tonight."

. . . *What if Bobby does talk to Tessa? The idea was scary. It would be so easy for Tessa to throw suspicion onto Penn. All she'd have to say is that she suspected Penn knew more about Laurie's death than he was telling.*

That would be enough to make Bobby try to beat the truth out of Penn.

I saw Bobby from my living-room window this afternoon. He was polishing his car with furious circular motions. I know that when he stared fiercely into its shiny surface, he wasn't thinking about his car. He was thinking about revenge.

Thirteen

Dear Diary,

Last night I dreamed we were up at the cabin. A fire was burning on the grate and the air was heavy with the smell of the colored chips Tessa liked to toss on the flames. In my dream, rose petals floated lightly in the air. I couldn't make out anyone's face, but I was sure we were all there—the cabin was full of people I loved.

I woke up with a shock when my alarm went off, and sat there shivering. I had once thought we all loved each other. "All for one and one for all," Tessa used to say. Friends forever. But now the cabin was gone, and Penn and I had to save ourselves. . . .

When Penn pulled up in front of the house at eight, I snatched up my book bag and ran out to him. I would be almost sorry to get my car out of the shop, it was so good to see him every morning.

"Why are you driving this way?" I asked when he backed out of the driveway and turned west. "Oh!" I said, understanding suddenly. Penn wasn't taking any chances about Stephen maybe lying in wait for us somewhere along our route with a rifle.

"I thought we'd go a different way," he said.

We drove out in the country. Birds swooped by the car. We passed a dilapidated tobacco barn. Penn knew his way around all the back roads.

"I talked to my dad when he came in last night," he said. I could hear a tone of suppressed excitement in his voice, and I glanced at him sharply. "Mrs. Landen is driving everybody at the office nuts," he said. "She's calling there all the time, saying she's having a heart attack and that she ought to go back to the hospital. Fact is, her heart's in rotten shape, but Dad says she doesn't need to be in the hospital." Penn grinned. "The real problem is that since she got out of the hospital, she's afraid to be on her own. He said she's called his emergency number every single night since she was discharged." We sped over a bridge, then through a stretch of woods.

"What does it have to do with us?" I asked, watching him closely. "Keep talking, Penn. You know I can't stand suspense."

"Dad thinks what she really needs is somebody to keep her company at night so she won't panic. He's already put in a call to the Home Health Services folks for a sitter, but they told him they've got a waiting list."

"Maybe she could go into a nursing home or a halfway house or something," I suggested.

"No!" Penn said, so loudly that I jumped. "This is our chance, Joanna. Don't you see? This may be the way out! This could be our way to escape the mess we're in."

I was puzzled. "I don't get it."

"Listen—I told my dad I knew a girl who'd be willing to stay with Mrs. L. at night for a few weeks."

"You did?" I said. A sick feeling swept over me. I could see now where this was leading.

"You could do it, couldn't you?"

"I don't know." I swallowed. "For one thing, I don't even know Mrs. Landen. She'd probably hate me. And she doesn't sound like the world's easiest person to get along with."

"It's only for a week or two," Penn pleaded. "And you wouldn't have to stay there alone. After the old lady goes to sleep, I'll slip in and stay the night."

"What have you got in mind? Are you thinking we'll scare Stephen off just by being there?"

"No! The last thing we want is to scare him off. What we want is for Stephen to think she's by herself. Mrs. L. hardly ever goes out anymore. That means if he wants to kill her, he's going to have to break into her house." Penn shrugged. "He probably thinks that would take care of it. An old lady with a weak heart—when he opens her bedroom door, chances are she'd have a heart attack on the spot."

"*I'll* probably have a heart attack." I pressed my palm to my chest.

"No you won't. I'll be right there beside you."

"What? How are you going to stop him?"

Penn shot me a pitying look. "I'm going to have a gun."

The car bumped over some railroad tracks and the landscape began to look more familiar.

"I don't know, Penn," I said uneasily.

"I could shoot low and hit him in the leg. He won't expect gunfire because he won't even know I'm there." Penn smiled. "A wounded housebreaker on the scene. Me, you, Mrs. Landen, and half the neighborhood would be witnesses that Stephen broke in. It's legal to shoot somebody who breaks into a house at night, you know."

"What if you kill him?" I asked.

A muscle jerked at the corner of his eye. "I'm not going to kill him," he said abruptly.

"No," I agreed. I could see that my question had upset him. "If it's dark, you probably won't even hit him."

"It's the only chance we've got, Joanna. And just think how great it will be if it comes off. Stephen gets locked up. You and I get a decent night's sleep for the first time in months."

It seemed to me that there were a lot of possible hitches in Penn's plan. Almost too many to list.

"Look at it this way," he went on before I could object. "Do you have a better plan?"

I didn't. I couldn't think of any other plan at all. I took a deep breath. "Okay," I said. "Let's do it."

. . . How can we be sure Stephen is going to break into Mrs. Landen's house? Penn's plan seems like such a long shot. But I keep remembering Tessa slipping that envelope into

her purse. Maybe it's not such a long shot after all. Penn's right. Stephen won't dare wait long. If he plans to kill Mrs. Landen, he'll want to kill her soon—before she talks.

Tessa thinks she's done Stephen a big favor by stealing that letter. It probably has never crossed her mind that she's put Mrs. Landen in danger. How can she be so stupid?

So much can go wrong! Penn and I could get shot, instead of Stephen. Anything can happen when guns are going off in the dark. It's a crazy scheme! I can't believe we're seriously considering it.

I would never go along with Penn's plan if I weren't desperate. But what are our other choices? We can turn ourselves in to the police or we can sit around waiting for Stephen to kill us. With choices like that, Penn's crazy idea starts to look good. . . .

Fourteen

My father thought my new part-time job staying with an old lady was a good idea. He always liked anything that kept me out of his way. "It won't interfere with your schoolwork, I hope," he said perfunctorily. He was sorting through the junk mail while we spoke.

"I'll have lots of time to study at night," I said. "Besides, I've already gotten into State. What I make on final exams doesn't much matter."

"True," he said. "Well, taking care of the old lady might be a good experience for you. Maybe it'll turn out you want to be a nurse or something like that."

"Maybe so," I said, keeping my face carefully expressionless.

I got my car back from the shop that afternoon. The shiny new windshield still had a sticker attached to one corner. I threw my knapsack in the trunk, tossed my overnight bag in after it, and drove to Mrs. Landen's.

She lived in a small, neatly kept shingle house with blue shutters. The street, which sloped up an incline, was quiet, with no signs of life. Vines climbing up the mailboxes. Greenacre Lane was in one of the older neighborhoods my dad had pointed out on the map for me when he was proving that the gunshot that shattered my windshield couldn't have come from a hunter's gun.

I stood on the tiny front porch and rang the bell. At the top of the steps was a potted cactus with hairlike spikes. I hoped the plant wasn't a clue to the personality of the owner. The front door was inset with four panes of glass, but I couldn't see into the living room because a thin white curtain covered the window.

At last the front door opened a bit and a pair of watery blue eyes regarded me with suspicion.

"Mrs. Landen?" I inquired. "I'm Joanna Rigsby. I've come to stay with you. Dr. Parrish arranged it?"

The door opened wider then, and I saw she was leaning on a gleaming chrome cane. Her hair was iron-gray in a tight perm, her nose was thin, and her earlobes were long and fleshy. The fingers of her left hand were encrusted with diamond rings with gray-looking settings. I walked past her into the room, being careful not to bump against her cane.

"It's quiet here, and there isn't much for you to do," she said in a loud, toneless voice. "You can get a lot of studying done."

Once a teacher always a teacher, I thought. "I'll bring in my suitcase and my book bag later," I said.

Mrs. Landen glared. "Mumbling is a very bad habit," she said. "You should enunciate each word clearly and distinctly."

I remembered that she was hard of hearing and raised my voice to a shout. "My suitcase and book bag are outside. I'll go get them."

"You don't have to shout," she said irritably. "I'm not deaf, only a little hard of hearing. If you will only speak up and not mumble, you will do fine."

The tiny living room was separated from the dining room by a shelf with a collection of porcelain figurines—smirking shepherdesses, nesting bluebirds. A spinet was pushed up against one wall; its top was covered with a lace scarf and a thick jumble of photographs in silver frames. A few small pieces of furniture filled the room almost to crowding. Under the shelf was a round-backed chair upholstered in a dull satin with a vaguely Oriental design. A Victorian love seat with a flame-stitched pattern sat next to it.

Mrs. Landen led me back to my room, which turned out to be a pleasant surprise. It was sunny, with sliding glass doors that opened onto a deck in back. The bed was covered with a quilted satin bedspread. A double bed, I noticed with a sigh of relief. Penn would not have to sleep on the floor after all. The sliding glass doors of the room would be handy for letting him in at night. The bedroom even had its own bathroom, so I wouldn't have to share with Mrs. Landen. "This was my daughter's room," explained Mrs. Landen. "I hope you don't watch a lot of television. When mine broke, I didn't bother to get it fixed. The sound quality is so poor these days, you can hardly hear what anyone is saying. And the shows are vulgar. I have no patience with them."

"It's okay," I shouted. "I don't watch much TV, and I need to study for finals anyway."

She beamed, her face falling into tiny wrinkles around her eyes and mouth. "Dr. Parrish told me you were a very studious, reliable girl. I have a feeling this is going to work out nicely. Would you care for a glass of iced tea?"

I shook my head, smiling. "I'll go get my things now," I shouted.

I felt a twinge of guilt as I went to get my things out of the car. Mrs. Landen had no clue that I expected a prowler to break into her house, nor that Penn would be sleeping with me. We were using the old lady as bait, and that bothered me. I liked to think of myself as a basically good person, but every day seemed to bring new proof that I wasn't as good a person as I thought. A sneering little voice inside told me that all I really cared about anymore was Penn's and my coming out of this alive.

When I got back to the house with my bags, Mrs. Landen sat down on the Victorian love seat and put a glass of iced tea on a cork coaster on the table beside her. Condensation beaded and streaked down the sides of the glass. "Have a seat," she commanded. "You can put your things away later."

I dropped my bags and sat down next to her on the love seat. It was easier than arguing.

"Dr. Parrish told me that you and his son are sweethearts. Is that true?" She didn't give me a chance to answer, but kept talking in a loud, toneless voice. "I taught Penn in the ninth grade. I remember Penn very well. Such a handsome boy. Hard to get to know, a trifle reserved for such a young boy—but smart. He could do the work, all right. I told Dr. Parrish, that boy will go far if he will only put his mind to it."

I smiled so hard, I was afraid my face would break. Mrs. Landen's years in teaching had gotten her used to having a captive audience. I expect she missed the nonstop monologues of the classroom.

"I got out of teaching just in time," she said, a tinge of regret in her voice. "Students today don't show the respect for teachers that they used to. And the violence! Someone told me that just the other day a student was shot at right in front of the high school!"

My smile froze on my face.

"Why, when I was a girl, chewing gum in class was the biggest disciplinary problem we had. We never had any of these guns and drugs. Terrible." She braced her hands on her knees. "But I'm sure you don't want to hear me go on about world problems. Very boring for you. Where are you planning to go to college?"

"State!" I shouted, muttering to myself, "If I live that long."

She looked hurt. "You don't have to shout. I heard you perfectly. State is a good school, though I hear some students complain that the classes are too large. Just a word of advice. Many of your classmates from Barton will go to State, but remember that college is a time to expand your horizons. You want to meet all sorts of people. You must be careful you don't hang around with your old friends too much."

I could feel hysterical laughter bubbling inside me. I faked a bout of heavy theatrical coughing to cover it up.

"Are you sure you won't have some tea?" asked Mrs. Landen, concerned.

The phone rang loudly in the kitchen. "I'll get it!" I cried.

Mrs. Landen's face registered relief. "I've thought about having that phone taken out. The connections are so poor that half the time I can't hear what people are saying." She continued to talk as I moved through the dining room to the kitchen. "All I seem to get is telephone solicitors anyway, but I feel I should keep it for emergencies. I do on rare occasions need to call Dr. Parrish to ask him a few questions."

I stuck my head out the kitchen door and shouted, "It's for me!" then ducked back into the kitchen at once. "Hi," I said, melting with relief at the sound of Penn's voice. "It's so good to hear from you!"

"Are you alone?" he asked. "Can Mrs. Landen hear what you're saying."

"Don't worry about that!" I said. "She'd be lucky to hear the house falling in. She's deaf; she's got arthritis and has to walk with a stick. And she's got liver spots on the backs of her hands. Getting old is so awful!"

"You and I may not have to worry about it."

I felt a cold clutch in my stomach.

"Are you still there?" Penn asked.

"Still here. It's just that I'm about to pass out from fright." I glanced around me. The kitchen was small and old-fashioned but spotless. Nothing had been left on the Formica counters. The small refrigerator did not even have refrigerator magnets. "Penn," my voice quavered, "it's not fair of us to set Mrs. Landen up like this."

"Getting cold feet?" he asked.

"*Major* cold feet."

"But I can't think of anything else to do. Can you?"

It was the unanswerable question. I had no other ideas. There was a silence, and finally I said, "Okay. Maybe this will work."

The kitchen was light and airy. Not only was there a window opening onto the deck, but sun came through the windows in the back door.

"This place is wide open, Penn," I said, eyeing the door uneasily. "He could break in the front door, the kitchen door, or the sliding glass door in my bedroom, and that's just a preliminary survey. The lady seems never to have heard of security. Not one door has a dead bolt on it."

"He's not going to break in the front," said Penn at once. "Somebody might see him."

"I bet everybody on this street goes to bed at eight."

"Yeah, but burglars never break in the front. What if a police car drove by? The main thing is, not to scare him off. That reminds me—put your car in the garage. If he sees you're there, he's going to know something is up."

"I'll see what I can do," I said.

"How are you and Mrs. L. getting on?"

"Oh, great. She's a sparkling conversationalist. She says you'll go far if you only put your mind to it."

"Me?" He was surprised. "Mrs. Landen's talking about me?"

"She and your father have jolly chats about

you. Or as jolly as possible, considering that she's stone deaf and only remembers you from the ninth grade."

"Well," said Penn grimly. "I got a gun today. Told the guy I was going to do some target practice. Which is true, by the way. I drove out to the cabin after school."

"Oh," I said faintly. I knew that must have been painful for him.

"Nothing left but the foundation now." His voice was emotionless. "I went out in the woods to the old outhouse and I did some target practice."

"Oh, Penn," I cried, "I don't think this is a good plan. Somebody could get hurt."

"That's the idea," he said.

"But what if it's one of us or Mrs. Landen?"

"One of us could get hurt if I don't do anything! This is all I could come up with. We've got to give it a try."

After I hung up, I went back in the living room. It was only a few steps away from the kitchen. Mrs. Landen had turned on the lamp beside her chair and was reading the *Evening Telegram*. "That was Penn," I shouted.

She smiled. "Sweet. Such a nice boy. So much like his father, and smart, too. He'll make a wonderful doctor."

I didn't bother to shout that Penn would rather be boiled in oil than be a doctor. What was the point? Since he was concentrating on simply staying alive, career ambitions seemed kind of superfluous. I smiled and nodded.

Suddenly a soft, explosive sound made me drop to the floor.

"Goodness, are you all right?" cried Mrs. Landen. "What happened? Did you trip?"

The lamp beside her had gone out. Blushing, I realized the sound I mistook for a muffled gunshot had only been a lightbulb blowing out.

I picked myself up off the floor. I'm sure my smile was strained. I felt as if my cheeks were full of Novocain. "I tripped!" I shouted. "Sorry!"

"You'd better move that bag to your room," said Mrs. Landen severely. "If I tripped over it, I might break a hip. I don't have your young bones."

I immediately took the knapsack to the bedroom. If an exploding lightbulb had me hitting the floor, I hated to think how I was going to handle real gunfire. On the other hand, I told myself, trying to look at the bright side, at least my reflexes were in good shape. I dumped the book bag, straightened my shoulders, and went back to the living room.

"And what do you plan to do with your life, Joanna?" Mrs. Landen looked at me with an air of intelligent interest as I sat down on the couch. She was probably thinking that I'd better scratch any career that had to do with being nimble on my feet.

I shrugged. "Not sure!" I yelled.

"Well, you're young yet," she said. "You have plenty of time for that."

Maybe I don't, I thought. "I thought I'd put my car in the garage," I shouted. "Is there room in there?"

Mrs. Landen looked surprised. "Don't you want to leave it parked on the street? It's so much easier. I always leave mine in the driveway."

"I just had to have a new windshield put in," I shouted. "I'd feel better if it were in the garage."

"It's not locked," she said. "But you may have to move some things to make room."

The garage was filled with dust-covered junk. It took me about a half hour, but finally I cleared a space. I thought I'd better drive in right away, before something fell down and I had to start all over again. I dusted myself off as best I could and went out to get my car. The sooner I got it hidden, the better. For all I knew, Stephen was casing the place this very afternoon.

I drove slowly. Just as I was pulling up to the back wall, however, I suddenly sneezed and reflexively my foot touched the gas pedal. The car gave a little bump, and something flashed past my windshield and hit the hood with a tinny thud. It was an old wicker baby carriage. It vibrated in tune with the motor, and its wire wheels spun.

I got out, carefully removed the carriage, and hooked it precariously on top of a lawn rake. Then I gently closed the garage door. I gazed with satisfaction at the closed garage door. It hadn't been easy, but I had done it. Now no one would guess that I was staying with Mrs. Landen unless they happened to see me come in or leave.

"Don't touch anything!" cried Mrs. Landen, horrified by my appearance when I returned. "And for heaven's sake don't touch the furniture."

I sneezed. "I guess I'd better wash up," I shouted.

Mrs. Landen nodded vigorously in agreement.

When I stepped out of the shower, I rubbed myself dry, wrapped a towel around my wet hair, dressed, and went back to the living room.

"I'd better do my homework now!" I shrieked.

"Oh my, yes. Don't let me keep you from your homework. Spread your work out wherever you like. There's plenty of room to work at the dining-room table."

The last thing I wanted was to try to study under Mrs. Landen's watchful eye. Instead of going into the dining room, I went back to my bedroom. There I took out all my school books and spread them out on the satin bedspread. But that was only in case Mrs. Landen peeked in. I had no interest at all in studying for finals.

Lately my personality seemed glued together entirely by fear. My ideas were few and simple—I was deeply grateful to be alive and out of jail. And I was determined to do my best to stay that way. I took off my shoes and walked softly around the room. I'm not sure why I was so careful to be quiet. Mrs. Landen certainly couldn't hear me.

I pulled a book out of the bookshelf and I threw myself belly down on the bed. I could never resist checking out other people's books. That was how I had happened to stumble on the book Laurie had once given Bobby. "To Bobby, with all my heart and soul forever. Laurie," it had said in a rounded script. What had surprised me at the time was that the inscription was so passionate. It didn't seem quite the right tone for a message from a stepsister to her stepbrother. Now I took it for granted that Bobby and Laurie had been in love. All that astonished me was that Laurie had thought of giving Bobby a book.

I opened the glossy book. It was the 1963 annual for Barton City High. It fell open to the P's and my eye lit on a faintly familiar face—Penn's father! He was skinny and was wearing horned-rimmed glasses, his jaw jutting determinedly at the photographer's camera. Ben Parrish. Math Club. Band. Science Club. Most Studious. A nerd, I thought, smiling. Well, he showed them. Now he's a rich cardiologist. But I thought I understood better why Penn's father had given him a Corvette. One part of him wanted Penn to study hard and be successful the way he was, but there must be some part of him that loved the idea of Penn having the glamour that he had never had.

I leafed through the yearbook aimlessly, vaguely surprised that the lunchroom help, the counselors, the principal, and the teachers were all unfamiliar. I thought of those people as permanent fixtures, like the brick buildings.

I flipped through the rest of the book until suddenly a name caught my eye. Tommy Dockerty. Math Club. Science Club. Astronomy Club. Most Intellectual. The one advantage of moving around so much during my high-school career was that at least I knew I wouldn't be elected Most Intellectual. I would have hated that. I gazed at the young version of Mr. Dockerty's face. Except for a certain thinning around the hairline, he hadn't changed much.

Dear Diary,

It was weird to look at that old yearbook, as if I had a telescope and could peer into the past. I had the odd sensation that the future is written down somewhere, too, if I only knew how to read it. Our new yearbook is due to come out any day now—at least, the yearbook staff keeps promising that it's on its way—and Laurie will be in it as well as Casey. But if there is a book of the future, then Laurie's and Casey's pages are blank. Dead people have no future.

Stephen, Tessa, Penn, and I are still alive. But it seems impossible to imagine that we'll all settle into being grown-ups with good jobs and families. Stephen working on his income tax? Tessa wiping the noses of toddlers? No, it can't happen. Why am I so sure of that? Is it because unconsciously I know that we, too, have no future?

Fifteen

. . . It's creepy to be in a strange house at night. Shadows move on the deck and make me gasp. It's only the wisteria vine swaying in the breeze, I tell myself. But this sensible explanation doesn't quiet my heart. Close by a bird chirps and makes me jump. I hope Penn will come soon. What if Stephen is trying to break into the house right now?

I started when I heard a tapping on the glass of the sliding door. A strangely ominous figure stood tall and threatening in the shadows on the deck, and it took me a minute to see that it was Penn. I slid off the bed at once and unlocked the door. To my relief, once he stepped into the bedroom, by the light of its cozy pink ruffled boudoir lamps, he looked like himself again. His hair was blown, and he smoothed it with one hand as he tossed a tote bag to the floor. When he enfolded me in his arms, I was shocked by the coldness of his hands. "Where did you put your car?" I asked.

"A block over, behind a convenience store. Is Mrs. Landen asleep yet?"

"She's been asleep for hours. We had a cup of Ovaltine together at nine; then she took her bath and I tucked her in."

"Mmm, you smell good." He kissed me.

I glanced over my shoulder uneasily. "Where's the gun?"

Penn bent to unzip the tote bag and took out a heavy-looking pistol.

"Where are you going to put it?" I asked.

Penn looked around. "On the bedside table, don't you think?" It clanked against the wood when he laid it down. "I want to be able to get at it fast," he said. It looked strange there next to the plump porcelain lamp with the pink ruffled shade.

I regarded it with horror. "How can we be sure it won't go off?"

"It's got a safety catch."

I threw a glance over my shoulder. I could not

escape the feeling Mrs. Landen might walk in any minute. "Maybe we'd better lock the bedroom door," I said.

"We can't," said Penn. "We've got to leave the door cracked so we'll see him if he comes through the kitchen."

"What if Mrs. Landen looks in here and sees you?" I cried. "She'd have a fit!"

"She's not going to see me," said Penn. "The lights are going to be out, remember? Calm down."

I sat down by the dressing table, my eyes drawn magnetically to the gun by the lamp. "How can you expect me to be calm when I'm waiting for a murderer to break into the house?" A roaring in my ears made me wonder if I might pass out. I gasped for breath. I had thought that once Penn arrived, I would feel more calm. Instead, the sight of the gun lying beside the little pink lamp filled me with panic.

"I'm not going to change clothes," Penn said. "I don't want to be chasing a burglar in my pajamas." He plucked a toothbrush from his bag and stepped into the bathroom. I could hear sounds of running water and vigorous brushing and gargling. When he came out, he kissed me noisily on the neck. I froze at his touch, and he pulled away, hurt. "What's the matter?" he asked.

"I keep thinking Mrs. Landen's going to walk in any minute," I said.

Penn threw back the bedspread. "Gee," he said lightly, "I can tell that staying over here is going to be a lot of fun."

I sat down on the bed and tugged off my shoes.

"Don't forget to crack the door," Penn reminded me.

I pulled the door open about six inches, then scurried back to the bed, goose bumps rising on my arms.

"You're a light sleeper," said Penn. "We should hear him all right."

When we switched off the lamps, for a second colored pinwheels spun before my eyes. "You really think he's going to come in the kitchen door?" I whispered.

"Yeah. That makes the most sense. He could put tape on those panes in there and then he could break them and reach in without making much noise. It would maybe sound like breaking eggs. But the sliding glass door is too big to break using tape. It'd make a huge racket."

The moonlight shed a thin radiance on the

deck, and the lacy shadows of the wisteria moved in the breeze. "Penn," I whispered. "If he comes in through the sliding glass door, he's going to see there are two people in the bed."

Penn's teeth flashed white in the darkness. "So what? He'll think Mrs. L. has a lot more exciting life than he figured."

I shivered. "I've got an idea. Why don't we sleep under the bed? He'd never see us then."

Penn snorted. "Forget that. For one thing, we'd be sneezing and bumping our noses on the box springs all night, and for another, we'd never get out from under there in time to catch him. Look, quit worrying about it. All you're doing is scaring yourself to death."

He was right. I needed to get some sleep. I stared at the shadowy ceiling. The deck outside was luminous with moonlight, and shadows moved in the room. My jeans seemed to have a hundred seams pressing into my flesh. It annoyed me that Penn was so cool, and suddenly I rolled over and punched him. "Hey," he protested. "Don't do that. Remember, I'm an armed man."

"How can you be so calm," I said tearfully, "when I'm totally freaking out?"

"Lift up your head," he commanded. A bit awkwardly, he slid his arm under my neck and pulled me close. His warm breath whistled close to my ear as he nuzzled me. "Didn't you ever play cops and robbers when you were a kid?" he said softly. "It's like that. It doesn't seem real to me yet."

I snuggled close to him, resting my head in the hollow of his shoulder. "I wish it weren't real. I wish this *were* a game."

"Go to sleep," he said softly. "It's going to be all right."

I was comforted in spite of myself. Before I knew it I had fallen asleep.

The alarm's buzzer went off at seven. I slid out of bed at once, clicked the bedroom door closed, and pushed in the lock. At least now I could breathe easily without worrying that Mrs. Landen would somehow walk in on us. Penn kicked the covers off, rolled over, and stretched with a groan.

"Hush!" I cried. "Mrs. Landen might hear you."

He sat up and reached for his shoes. "I have a feeling I'm going to get awfully tired of hearing that line."

I sighed and plopped back down on the bed. I noticed that the gun beside the porcelain lamp was beginning to look normal to me. Maybe it really is true that you can get used to anything. "Anyway, there's been no sign of Stephen yet," I said.

"Not yet. But this is only day one. Don't give up hope." Penn put his arm around me. "I'm out of here. Give me a kiss."

I heard the sound of water running. A toilet had flushed. "She's awake." I stiffened.

"Jeez," groaned Penn. "I guess we'd better get up earlier." He ran his fingers through his hair and grabbed his tote bag. "Bye," he said. He slid the glass door open and slipped out. I saw him toss the bag over the deck railing and vault lightly over it. He landed with a soft thud and a rustle of leaves. I was glad he hadn't risked walking by the kitchen window—Mrs. L. could already be in there.

I opened the glass door, leaving the screen pulled closed to keep out mosquitoes. Beyond the deck, shafts of sunlight stirred in the trees. The leaves rustled, and somewhere a dog was barking. I hoped none of the neighbors saw Penn slinking through their backyards this morning.

After the fitful anxious sleep of the night before, the sunny morning with the trill of birds' songs seemed like a miracle. I hummed a tune as

I washed my face and changed clothes. In the bathroom mirror I noticed faint shadows smudged under my eyes.

Mrs. Landen was in the kitchen, a plaid bathrobe wrapped around her shapeless form. She was measuring out a teaspoon of instant coffee. "Good morning!" she boomed. Her face was creased and papery, as if she had dried out overnight. "I hope you slept well. I don't sleep as well as I used to, myself. I take sleeping pills, but they don't work."

"Oh, I slept fine," I said. Then, remembering she couldn't hear me, I shouted, "Fine!"

When I got to school, I looked around for Stephen and Tessa, but they weren't in their favorite dark stairwell. I checked Tessa's locker. Probably it looked no different from any of the other plain olive metal lockers that lined the walls, but to me it looked unused and deserted. Worry was beginning to gnaw at me.

I saw Bobby sitting on the edge of a brick planter, scraping clay off the encrusted soles of his sneakers with a Popsicle stick. "Bobby, have you seen Tessa?"

He looked up. "Heck no. You looking for her?"

"Sort of."

"I thought you two weren't speaking." He stabbed the Popsicle stick into the ground. "I called over at her house, but some little kid picked up the phone and I couldn't make out what he was saying. So I hung up."

I gave a fake laugh. "You aren't still thinking you're going to ask Tessa about that stupid fight we had, are you?"

"Naw," said Bobby, with heavy sarcasm. "I'm gonna ask her for a date. Come on! What do you think I'm doing? I'm going to get to the bottom of this thing. And don't think you can stop me."

"Did I try to stop you?" I asked, eyeing him apprehensively.

"You're acting pretty funny, seems to me." He scowled at me.

"If somebody shot at you, you might be acting funny, too." I edged away from him. "Well, if you see Tessa, tell her I'm looking for her."

What on earth would I say to Tessa if I found her? I wondered. It wasn't so much that I wanted to see her as that I was afraid to let her out of my sight. Maybe if we met up, I could be super friendly. As if our little chat in the girls' room had never happened. I didn't think I was going to run into her, though. More and more I was convinced that she and Stephen weren't at school.

At lunchtime, when I got to the cafeteria, Penn was at our usual table.

"Have you seen Stephen or Tessa?" I asked, sliding my chair up to the table.

The air smelled strongly of overcooked spaghetti sauce.

Penn smiled wryly. "No, since you ask, I haven't seen Stephen or Tessa all day. What are you getting at?"

My thumbs gripped the edge. "Penn, what if they're halfway to Mexico by now? Wouldn't that be great?"

His fingers tapped nervously on the table. "That would be something, all right," he said finally.

The moment stretched like taut elastic between us. Around us the raucous noises of the cafeteria, the clatter of trays and dishes, the laughter and the chatter seemed to swell to an indistinct roar.

"Maybe Mrs. Landen's letter made them panic," I said.

"I can't believe Tessa would take off for Mexico." Penn bit his lip thoughtfully. "You know how she's got her heart set on going to Princeton."

"Stephen could get her to do anything he wanted," I said.

"Maybe. But he didn't get her to go to Rutgers with him."

"Maybe he didn't ask," I suggested.

"Oh, he asked." Penn's eyes met mine. "He was kidding, you know, but serious, too. He told me. But she blew it off." He threw his fork onto his plate with a noisy clatter. "It doesn't make sense! Why would Tessa run? She's still saying Stephen hasn't done anything really wrong. If he wanted her to go with him, he'd have to tell her the truth."

We stared at each other for a long minute.

"I'm not sure he'd be smart to do that," I said.

"You're right," said Penn. "I think Tessa'd find it hard to swallow two cold-blooded murders. So it's a no go. Tessa won't run, and we know Stephen won't go without her."

"So where are they, then?" I cried.

"Probably they're skipping school," said Penn. "They could even be at the beach, for that matter. Why not?"

I took a deep breath. "Won't you even let me hope they've caught a deadly virus and infected each other?"

Sixteen

After school I went home to pick up some clothes. I fixed myself a peanut-butter-and-jelly sandwich—I hadn't eaten any lunch—then drove to Mrs. Landen's house. The dimpled surface of the car's steering wheel was warm to my fingers. I switched on the radio and got a blast of country music—a somebody-done-somebody-wrong song. The spent azaleas along the side of the road drooped. It was another warm afternoon.

I was surprised when I drove up to the house to hear the deafening roar of a power mower. A huge sweaty fellow with a red bandanna wound around his head was mowing the small front yard. I could see the muscles of his freckled shoulders bulging as he pushed the mower up an incline in front of the hedges. Something about him was familiar.

I held my breath as I pulled the car into the garage. Fortunately I managed not to dislodge any of the junk piled up in the corners. I hoisted my book bag over one shoulder and went around to the front of the house. Grass clippings were flying and the air smelled of burned gasoline. The lawn worker had pulled the mower back, pivoting it around on its back wheels. He began mowing in my direction. I almost dropped my book bag when I realized that it was Bobby and that he had seen me. It was too late for me to get away, so I decided my best bet was to act friendly. His face was red and streaming with sweat. "You want a glass of water?" I shouted.

He cut off the mower, pulled the bandanna off his head, and mopped his face with it. "What'd you say?"

"I said, 'Do you want a glass of ice water?'"

"Sure," he said. "What are you doing over here?"

"I'm staying with Mrs. Landen. She gets nervous at night. What are you doing over here? I didn't know you mowed lawns."

"I don't. Not exactly. Hey, don't forget that water."

I dropped my knapsack beside the couch, went into the kitchen, and filled a tumbler with ice and water. My mind was whirring. Had Bobby followed me to Mrs. Landen's?

There was no sign of Mrs. Landen. I figured she must have been taking an afternoon nap. Nobody else could have slept with the roar of that power mower outside, but Mrs. Landen could do it.

Outside I found Bobby sitting on the steps, his head drooping between his knees. I handed him the water. "You were going to tell me what you're doing here," I reminded him.

He threw back his head and took a long drink of water. "My mother makes me mow Mrs. Landen's lawn, and man, she always picks the hottest day of the week. It never fails."

I regarded him narrowly. "You mean you've done this lawn mowing before? You haven't just started?"

"For years," he groaned. "And get this. Mrs. Landen thinks she's doing me a big favor when she pays me five bucks."

Odd—I had never figured Bobby for a philanthropist.

"My mom feels sorry for her," Bobby went on. "She keeps telling me Mrs. Landen doesn't have any friends and we need to help her out. It's a bunch of baloney, but it's easier for me to come over here and mow the stupid lawn than to argue."

"That's very sweet of you, Bobby."

He growled, "I told you, my mom makes me do it."

"Well, anyway . . ."

He handed me the empty glass and went glowering back to the lawn. With narrowed eyes I watched him start the mower. Was he telling me the truth? Or was he only making up an excuse to be here keeping an eye on me?

When I went inside, I found Mrs. Landen sitting in her favorite chair, with a bowl of potato chips in her lap. She was reading a magazine, and a tall glass of iced tea stood on the table beside her.

"Has Bobby finished the lawn yet?" she asked querulously. "I want to be sure to pay him. The last time, he went off without getting his money, and I had to mail it to him. It was a lot of extra trouble."

"He's not quite finished," I shouted. "He only stopped to drink a glass of water."

"Go out and remind him to get up close around the azaleas. People are so slapdash these days." Mrs. Landen frowned. "I wrote to the principal at the high school days ago. I certainly thought I would have heard by now, wouldn't you?"

"The mail is pretty slow," I shouted.

"I remember when you could send a letter for three cents and it'd arrive the next day. Nowadays, I do believe they route the local mail through Houston. Maybe I should have you call the school, Joanna."

I was thrown for a moment. That move made sense, but it wasn't exactly part of Penn's plan. "It's after four," I pointed out. "The school is closed."

Mrs. Landen glanced at her watch. "You're right. Imagine me forgetting that," she said irritably. "Well, there's no help for it. It's probably better to write the man another letter anyway. It's too provoking! Do you know Stephen Garner?"

I sat down suddenly. My knees felt weak. "Yes, ma'am," I said faintly. "I do."

"Speak up, Joanna," she snapped. "You know how it irritates me when you mumble."

"Yes, I know Stephen," I shouted. My face felt cold, as if all the blood had somehow congealed in my heart.

"The oddest thing happened," she said in her

loud, toneless voice. "I saw in the paper that he was second in the graduating class. Of course, I knew at once there had to be some mistake, because I had given him a C in my course. His research paper was not up to his usual standard of work. It was pedestrian and the topic was not clearly defined. I remember it quite well, because he got very angry with me about the grade. Such an impertinent boy!" Pink spots of color rose in her slack cheeks. "'Don't talk to me in that tone of voice, young man,' I told him. 'Nothing you say will influence me in the slightest, and if you're thinking of getting your parents to come up here and complain, then think again.'"

I was so riveted by what she was saying that I didn't even notice that the sound of the power motor had stopped until Bobby rapped on the door. I jumped up at once and opened the door.

"Hand me my purse, Joanna," said Mrs. Landen.

I got her twill-cotton purse off the piano stool and handed it to her. She groped in its cavernous interior. "Joanna, before I pay him, you'd better go out and check to be sure he's gone carefully around the azaleas."

I shot Bobby an embarrassed look. He turned around without a word and went outside. He had taken off his bandanna and, teeth clenched, was twisting it between his hands in a strangling motion. "Can you believe that old biddy?" he said in a choked voice.

"What azaleas am I supposed to check?" I asked nervously.

He gestured to a line of plants along the low chain-link fence that separated Mrs. Landen's front yard from the neighbor on her west. "If I get any closer to them, it's going to be bye-bye azaleas," he said. "What does she expect me to do? Go around the bed with fingernail clippers?"

"Looks okay to me," I said at once.

Bobby gave me a disgusted look. "For crying out loud. What does she think I am?"

"She's old," I said apologetically.

"She's not *that* old. I bet she's been a pain in the neck her whole life. You notice her daughter lives halfway around the world. You don't think that's an accident, do you? Mrs. Landen's just lucky nobody's murdered her."

I couldn't keep myself from jumping at the word "murdered," and Bobby regarded me with a look of open suspicion. He stepped up close to me. I could feel his hot breath on my face. "What's the matter with you, Jo? What are you freaking out about? And what are you and the old lady talking about in there? Something about Stephen?"

I realized that as loudly as we had been talking, Bobby must have heard every word. I wished I knew how long he had been listening.

"Stephen was in her class once," I said, my hands working nervously. "She didn't like him much."

He snorted. "I said she was mean. I didn't say she was stupid. Naturally she didn't like him. I don't like him either. But what's this junk about his research paper?"

"I don't know, Bobby. You know how she is. She drones on and on about the old days. I think Stephen talked back to her or something."

"And that's all there is to it?"

I shrugged. "That's all."

"Then how come you look so jumpy, like you're about to go up in smoke any minute?"

I closed my eyes. "Staying with Mrs. Landen is not a relaxing experience, Bobby. You ought to be able to understand that."

To my relief he seemed to accept my explanation. He cast a glance toward the house and said, "I'd better not go back in there. My mom wouldn't like it if I strangled an old lady."

"Don't leave without your five dollars!" I cried.

"Oh, come on!" His bloodshot eyes met mine. "Don't make me laugh."

"I'll get it for you." I darted inside the house. If the five dollars wasn't delivered to Bobby, I knew I'd be hearing about it all evening. When I returned, clutching the bill in my hand, Bobby was already climbing into his car. I held out the five dollars.

"Keep it," he said, slamming the door. A second later he roared off.

As I watched the car careen down the street, I stuffed the bill into my jeans pocket.

When I went back in the house, Mrs. Landen was fretful. "I wish I had asked him to trim the shrubbery while he was out here. I'm going to have to give his mother another call." She winced. "Would you get my arthritis medication, Joanna? It's on my bedside table."

Mrs. Landen's room was smaller than the one I was using and was scrupulously neat. The crisp white ruffled bedspread was piled high with little decorated pillows, their lace threaded through with fine strips of pale-blue ribbon. The medicine was on the bedside table, as she had said. Surveying the vast array of pill bottles, I realized that she was probably particularly out of sorts because her knees were bothering her. I thought about the old saying that you shouldn't judge a person until you have walked a mile in their moccasins and was glad I didn't have to walk a mile in Mrs. Landen's.

. . . With Mrs. Landen and me braying at each other at full volume, Bobby could have easily heard the entire story of Stephen's grade change. So far, I've been lucky. If only my luck holds out a little longer!

I called Tessa's house after Bobby left, simply to see if she was home. I guess I hoped to find out she had skipped town after all. I don't know what I would have said if she had come to the phone. Wrong number? But she didn't come to the phone. A small child answered the phone and instructed me in a singsong voice that Tessa had gone to the movies with Stephen.

So they haven't left town after all. I wonder what they're thinking of as they sit together in the darkened movie theater. Is Tessa doing her best to quiet her nagging doubts about what happened the day Laurie fell of the cliff? And what about the night the gun somehow went off in Stephen's hand and killed Casey? Stephen's hands have to be icy as they reach into the popcorn box. He knows that he's going to have to kill Mrs. Landen soon.

Seventeen

Dear Diary,

What a strange life I have these days! When I drive to school, I take elaborate evasive action. One route threads past an abandoned drive-in movie, its marquee still advertising an old X-rated movie. There's an odd bad-dream quality to driving on such out-of-the-way streets, streets that are the direct route to nowhere.

At midnight I let Penn in the sliding glass door at Mrs. Landen's. We doze fitfully under the pink satin bedspread until the buzzer of the alarm goes off at five thirty. I can feel the tension in Penn's body as he lies next to me. The game of cops and robbers has turned into a game of cat and mouse.

"He's got to make his move soon," Penn said last night. When I got up this morning, I noticed that a muscle has begun to twitch at the corner of Penn's eye. I'm afraid to look in the mirror for fear of what I'll see in my own face.

Thursday Penn didn't show up for lunch. I panicked and rushed to the pay phone in the lobby of the cafeteria. I was so rattled, I dropped my quarter and had to stoop to pick it up. I dialed his number and let it ring a long time, ten or twelve times, gripping the receiver tightly in my cold hand and willing him to answer. I was afraid he might be dead on the floor while the phone echoed unheard in the big house. Suddenly there was a click on the line. At first I was afraid I was disconnected, but then a slurred voice said, "Hello."

"Penn! What's wrong?" I cried.

"Headache," he said. "Awful headache. My dad gave me something for it." His voice trailed off.

I knew Penn sometimes got horrible headaches. It had happened before, when he found out Casey had gotten drunk at a party and was babbling in public about his illegal computer exploits.

"I'm coming over," I said.

"No. Don't. I'm going to sleep. I'll be okay."

"But, Penn," my voice quavered a little. "What about tonight?"

"I'll be there," he said. "Don't worry. I'll be there."

After I hung up, I stared blindly at the tile floor, feeling hopeless. What would I do if Penn didn't come? I didn't even have a gun. And if I had had one, it wouldn't have done me a bit of good. I couldn't shoot anyone—not even Stephen.

My footsteps echoed as I crossed the broad floor to the water fountain. I let the cold water splash my eyes. I have to get a hold on myself, I thought. Penn had promised to come as usual, and I had to assume that he would. If I weren't careful, I might blow the whole thing. It's important that I keep my nerve, I lectured myself sternly. I can't afford to panic. This is our only chance.

When I got to Mrs. Landen's, I was very careful to close the garage door after I parked my car so that Stephen couldn't see I was there.

"You're home!" said Mrs. Landen when I let myself in the house. "Don't you want a nice glass of tea or something?"

Her innocent pleasure in my company made

me feel queasy with guilt. I accepted the glass of tea she offered, and took a sip. It was flavored with artificial sweetener and so full of cooked lemon juice that it made my mouth pucker.

"Can you type, Joanna?"

I nodded.

"This morning I had an idea. Do you remember that letter I wrote to the school? Instead of writing it out longhand, I could dictate what I want to say and you could type it for me."

She led me to a nearby room, where a dress form stood in one corner. A sewing machine sat in front of the window. Next to it, on a typing table, was the oldest typewriter I had ever seen, all spidery bits of metal and keys that looked like insect legs with beige key covers. "This is the typewriter I used in college," said Mrs. Landen proudly.

I typed out a rough draft of the letter as she dictated it to me.

"I'll have to type up a good copy of this," I shouted when I was done. "Then you can sign it." I could hear a humming noise, and I turned involuntarily to stare at the typewriter, wondering if it had suddenly metamorphosed into an IBM electric, but it was still the same antique.

Mrs. Landen was reading over my shoulder.

"Having you type it was a good idea," she said. "When you get the final copy done, I'll proofread it and sign it."

The buzzing noise grew louder. I pulled up the blinds to peer outside and found myself staring at Bobby's grimacing face. Startled, I dropped the blinds shut.

"Oh, good," said Mrs. Landen, sounding pleased. "Bobby's already working on the shrubbery. Go out there and make sure he's getting it straight, Joanna."

"I don't think he likes my checking on him," I shouted.

"I don't care whether he likes it or not," said Mrs. Landen. "I'm the one who's paying him. I'd check on him myself if I could get around a little better."

Resigned, I went outside. Bobby switched off the electric hedge clippers. "Coming out here with a tape measure?" he asked sarcastically.

I sat on the steps. "Looks real good to me."

"Who got you this job, anyway?" he asked.

"Who? Me?" I asked, staring at him with startled eyes.

"Yeah. You. You don't even know old crabby-nose. What are you doing over here?"

"Well, she needed somebody to stay with her

at night for a while. It's her nerves, mostly."

"That's not what I asked you," said Bobby in a hard voice. "What I want to know is, who sent you and why are you here?"

I felt hot color rush to my head. He looked at me so coldly that for an awful instant I had the feeling he knew the whole truth.

"I've got to go," I said nervously. "I'd better check on Mrs. Landen."

"Hey, wait a minute," protested Bobby. He put a hand on my shoulder, but I shook him off.

"Really," I said. "I've got to go."

I should have simply told him that Penn's dad had gotten me the job, I thought miserably as I closed the front door behind me. I had handled it badly and only ended up making him more suspicious, but I panicked when he started asking questions. Why did he have to keep hanging around watching me?

The scene with Bobby replayed in my mind that night when I showered and brushed my teeth. I knew that everything about me must seem suspicious. My eyes stared at the mirror, wide and alarmed. The sharpness of my cheekbones almost showed through my flesh—when was the last time I had eaten a full meal? I couldn't remember. I was sure that I looked guilty. No wonder Bobby tagged after me and asked me questions.

For the first time, I was sorry the television wasn't working. I desperately needed to watch something stupid, something with a laugh track. Otherwise there was nothing to do but gaze out the sliding glass door and wait for Penn. None of the books on the bedroom bookshelf could keep my attention. Uneasiness crawled just under my skin. I was unbearably restless. Then I noticed that an ancient hardcover book had gotten pushed behind the others. Taking out a couple of the paperbacks that were in front of it, I pulled out the hardcover—it was so old that the title had worn off the spine—and opened to the title page. *How to Stop Worrying and Start Living.* The book fell open, and my eye lit on a line in bold print: "Ask yourself, 'What's the worst that can happen?'" I shut the book abruptly and shoved it back behind the other books where I had found it. The last thing I needed to do now was to imagine the worst that could happen. Even thinking of the best that could happen was making me fall apart.

I turned out the light and slid under the

covers. Outside, the wind rustled through the trees with a sound like silk skirts brushing along a floor. The night was ominously overcast, and I could hear dry leaves noisily skidding along the deck. The blackness was profound. The luminous dial of the alarm clock told me that it was after midnight. Penn was late.

A pulse was throbbing in my throat so hard, it seemed it might choke me. Should I call him? I wasn't sure I could speak. All I could think of was that the kitchen was where Penn had said Stephen was probably going to break in. If I went into the kitchen now, I might see his face in the shadows by the back door.

The wind rose in the trees like a sigh, and then, so softly I could scarcely hear it, rain began to fall. I must have dozed off, because I woke up with a start to a confused impression of a noise like shattering glass. My hand gripped the bedspread and I felt a sharp pain and wetness. The glass door had shattered! In a quick motion I slipped from under the covers and rolled under the bed. The crosspieces of wood under thin muslin pressed against the tip of my nose, and my nostrils tickled. My hand burned—somehow I had cut it.

Now the darkness was different—windy, and damp. The swishing of the trees was louder. And I heard a more ominous sound, the crunch of glass under a footstep. Under the weight of a shoe, the glass cracked with a sharp snapping sound and then a crunch. I heard a soft brushing and scraping, and realized the intruder must be scuffing his shoes on the carpet to get the broken glass off. Then came a crash and a tinkling sound. Glass was still falling out of the door. I was glad of the noise, because the sound of my breathing seemed impossibly loud. I held my breath and willed myself not to sneeze. The floor vibrated under me with the intruder's footsteps. When I rolled my eyes to the right, I saw sneakers and smelled the distinctively smoky smell of Stephen's jeans. I heard a click and suddenly the white toes of his sneakers were inches away from me, illuminated by the glow of a flashlight that was now playing over the room. Staring unblinking at the shoes inches from my eyes, I saw him rock slightly. His weight had shifted. He must be about to take a step. I was afraid even to swallow.

A hawking dry cough sounded in the next room. It was Mrs. Landen! One sneaker stepped back so that I couldn't see it. Dead silence. Then I felt the vibration of his steps as he walked from the bed. He was on his way to the other room.

Stephen was going to kill Mrs. Landen!

Eighteen

I lay under the bed, panicking. Somehow I had to stop Stephen from murdering the innocent old woman. But what could I possibly do? In seconds he would be in Mrs. Landen's room.

I scooted part of the way out from under the bed and reached for the phone. Carefully muffling it in my hand, I pulled it down to the floor. I felt for the 9 on the dial—the second-to-last hole—and rotated it clockwise. My fingers were slick with blood, and the soft whine of the dial whirring back to place seemed loud to my ears, but Mrs. Landen was coughing again and I thought Stephen might not have heard me. My fingers walked to the other end of the rotary dial, desperately feeling for the 1. I couldn't afford a wrong number. Rigid with fear, I listened to the phone ring at the other end. I seemed to hear blood roaring in my eardrums. I knew he must be standing in front of Mrs. Landen's room listening.

"This is the police," said a cheerful voice.

"Three-oh-two Greenacre Lane," I said distinctly. "Burglar. Hurry." I knew Stephen had heard me now. I laid down the receiver. I could hear a tiny electronic voice coming from the receiver asking me to repeat the address. I strained my ears but I heard only silence. Stephen must have been standing very still, trying to fix where my voice had come from. He hadn't expected me to be here. That I was on the floor and that the small electronic sound had followed my voice might be momentarily confusing. But I was sure of one thing—when he came for me, I didn't want to be trapped under the bed.

I jerked the phone out of the wall in a smooth motion as I rolled out from under the bed and leapt breathlessly to my feet. The phone jangled, and I expected a shot to ring out. Reflexively I cringed, but I was aware only that a figure somewhat lighter than the blackness around it was blocking the doorway. I felt the floor shake—he was coming toward me!

Screaming, I heaved the phone at him. I groped for the porcelain lamp, blindly reaching behind me. Glass shattered and something warm and smoky brushed by me. A scream tore my throat. The room was crowded and confused; things tumbled off the dresser. A heavy tread crunched the broken glass underfoot.

"Joanna!" It wasn't the voice I expected, and I froze, confused. Someone yelped and uttered a string of oaths.

There was a sound of impact, body upon body, and a grunted "Oomph!"

"Are you okay? What the hell's going on?" It was Bobby's voice! I groped for the light switch, and Bobby, standing not three feet from me, blinked at me, his face befuddled. He glanced down. "Damn!" he said. "It's a cement block! Right in the middle of the bedroom."

"Get Stephen," I cried.

Bobby swore. "I tried to grab him, but he got away." He pivoted and ran limping out to the deck. "I see him," he cried.

I heard Bobby's heavy step on the deck and then nothing. On the floor, murderous-looking shards of glass winked ominously in the light. The satin bedspread had broken glass on it and a splash of blood. Blood had dropped on the carpet in a pattern like shaggy red coins. Sobbing, I groped in my bag for a T-shirt and pressed it against my bleeding hand. Then, crawling awkwardly over the bed to avoid the glass on the floor, I reached for the light switch and turned on the floodlights. A washed-out light illumined the deck, making the bare boards of the deck look bleak.

I sat on my knees on the bloodstained bedspread for several minutes, gasping for air. Then I forced myself to find my shoes and put them on. In the bathroom medicine cabinet I found some gauze pads and adhesive tape. I pressed the pad against the torn soft flesh at the base of my thumb and taped it tightly in place.

A faint cry came from Mrs. Landen's room. Mrs. Landen! I had forgotten about her! I hurried in to her and flicked on the light. Her watery blue eyes were wide and frightened, and she was gasping for air. I should have checked on her, I thought remorsefully. She must have been lying there in distress for several minutes, unable to make a noise.

"We've had a bit of excitement." My voice sounded shaky to my own ears. "But it's all over now. Everything's fine."

Mrs. Landen's chest was heaving under her white ruffled nightgown, but she didn't speak. "I'm going to call an ambulance," I said. I picked up the phone by her bed and dialed 911 again. Then I sat down on Mrs. Landen's bed and held her hand with my uninjured left hand. "It's going to be all right," I said in a soothing voice. "They're going to send an ambulance. You try to relax."

My eye was on the dial of her alarm clock. The second hand seemed to move with agonizing slowness. What if she died before the ambulance arrived? I went cold at the thought. I remembered the night Casey had died, the slackness of his face and the emptiness of his eyes. I wasn't sure I could face death again.

Mrs. Landen closed her eyes. The lids were bluish with veins, and papery thin. "I can't breathe," she gasped.

I realized suddenly that she hadn't been able to hear anything I had been saying. "The ambulance is on the way!" I screamed.

She nodded.

The seconds and the minutes crept by with agonizing slowness. It seemed to me her skin was turning a bluish color and that her breathing was unsteady.

"It shouldn't be long now!" I shrieked. "You take it easy. The ambulance'll be here soon." I heard a siren, but it stopped. Had I imagined it? I wondered frantically. Had I had gotten the address wrong when I talked to the 911 operator? Where were they? Why was it taking them so long? I picked up the phone and redialed.

"They're on their way, dearie," said the cheerful operator. "They've been delayed by an accident on the road."

I wanted to scream, but I thanked her and hung up, faking a smile to Mrs. Landen. "Not long now!" I shouted. "They're on the way."

In fact, it was another ten minutes before I heard the siren outside the house. "That's them!" I shouted. I jumped up and ran to the door. To my relief the two young paramedics had already wheeled a stretcher up onto the front porch.

"Thank goodness you're here," I said. "She's in the back bedroom." I stood aside to let them by.

"We'd have been here sooner, but a motorcycle collided with a police car up on the corner there and we had to stop and give first aid," said a curly-haired paramedic.

As the paramedic wheeled the stretcher into the hallway, it banged against the Victorian love seat. Mrs. Landen wouldn't like the gash in her sofa, but I couldn't worry about that now.

"Motorcycle accident?" I asked.

"Yeah. It was no use, though," the paramedic called behind him. "DOA."

I ran out the front door and into the yard. The ambulance loomed large in the driveway, its blue light flashing. I hurried around it. I could make out a flashing blue light through the trees, and I took off running toward it, stumbling over curbs and on the uneven sidewalks.

I was conscious of the heaviness of my legs, of the cool night air beating against my face and the sound of my running footsteps on the pavement. Breath tore painfully at my throat. It seemed to take forever to get up the rise at the end of the street. When I reached the top of it, gasping for breath, I saw Penn's Corvette pulled over to the side of the road, its lights on, and my heart stopped. Penn! What was he doing here?

Just around the corner were the flashing lights and the blazing headlights of police cars and another ambulance. Dark-clad men stood two and three together, silhouetted against headlights. The shifting red and blue lights gave the scene a nightmarish look. Stephen's motorcycle, lying flat on the side of the road, beamed a single headlight close to the ground. Blades of grass stood out in stark relief, and the bottom of a discarded soft drink can blazed like a silver disk.

It took me a while to realize that everyone was looking at the covered stretcher the paramedics were wheeling toward the ambulance. Someone was on the stretcher, his face covered with a sheet. His sneakers stuck out from under the sheet that covered him. When the medics slid the stretcher into the ambulance, I saw the glass in the soles glitter in the blue light. Stephen. DOA, the paramedic at Mrs. Landen's house had said. That meant dead on arrival. It seemed impossible. He had been warm and alive only minutes before when he had brushed past me in the bedroom.

It was only after they slammed the ambulance door shut behind the stretcher that I noticed Penn standing beside one of the police cars. He was swaying a little, and his hair had fallen in his face.

I ran over to him. "Are you okay?" I asked urgently, putting my arm around him. "Maybe you'd better sit down." To my surprise he immediately sat down on the ground, keeping his balance by hugging his knees. He looked stunned.

"He okay?" Bobby asked gruffly.

I jumped at the sound of his voice. I hadn't realized he had come up to us.

"I think he's woozy from pain medication," I

said. "His dad gave him something for a headache." I sat down on the ground next to him and touched his cheek gently with my finger. The damp from the wet ground seeped into my jeans.

"He's gone," Penn said hoarsely. I could barely hear him. "He's dead, Joanna."

"I took off after him," Bobby said, "but then somehow I lost him. Next thing I know I hear this big roar and I realize he's got a bike. He cuts right in front of me—I guess he had the bike hid behind a bush or something. I was so close, I guess I had this crazy idea I might catch him, and I took off, but already I could hear the police siren, and the next thing I know—bam! I heard the crash when he hit the cop car."

A police officer was walking toward us. "Can you talk to the police, Bobby?" I asked hastily. "I've got to get Penn home. You can see he's in bad shape."

Penn smiled ruefully and struggled to his feet. "Hey, I'm not out of my mind or anything. I can drive."

"No, I'll drive," I said. "Get in."

The police made no attempt to stop us. I climbed into the Corvette, slid the seat up, and took the keys from Penn's hand. He leaned his head back against the headrest. His pale face was blue in the flashing light of the police cars. "I don't know what my dad gave me," he groaned, "but he gave me too much. When I came to, I realized it was way past midnight. I got over here as fast as I could, but when I rounded the corner, the place was crawling with cop cars and there was an ambulance driving up." Suddenly his eyes opened wide and he looked at me. "They had left him there lying on the side of the road. His eyes were open and there was blood on his face!"

I felt a sick clutch in my stomach. Stephen! Could he really be dead? I eased the car down the incline and then turned into Mrs. Landen's driveway. "Let me lock up the house," I said. "I'll be right back."

A police car was parked in front of the house. I peeked my head in the open front door. "Hello?" I called. The house felt different—chill and airy. A police officer stepped out of the hallway. Another officer was close behind him.

"I've been staying with Mrs. Landen," I explained to them. "I'm the one who made the emergency call. But now that she's going to the hospital, I'm not planning to stay at the house. I've got to drive a friend home."

"We can't leave the place unsecured," one officer said heavily.

"I can lock it . . ." I began; then my voice trailed off. I remembered that the sliding glass door was smashed. A damp wind was blowing through the house. That was why it smelled different.

"We'll get some people to come over tonight and nail plywood over where the door was." The police officer hooked his thumbs on his belt loops. His potbelly strained at the fabric of his uniform, and his nose was round and shiny. He looked friendly and helpful, like an illustration in a child's book.

Dear Diary,

It's a shock to realize that I don't have to be afraid of the police. Stephen can't hurt us now—he's dead. He can't lie about Penn. He can't trap us in burning buildings or shoot at me. I know I should be happy, but instead I feel sick. Blood on his face, Penn said. I don't want to think about it.

Nineteen

Dear Diary,

It's weird to think that everything's changed now. The past couple of months had simple rules—don't talk to the police, don't betray friends, don't stand in the open within range of a sniper's shot. It was no fun, but there was nothing complicated about it. Now I have butterflies in my stomach and a vague sense of uneasiness. I keep wondering what might happen next. . . .

Penn let us in the back door at his house. His father was sitting in the kitchen in his robe. His skin was stretched tight over the bones in his face, and his eyes had sunk deeply into his eye sockets.

"Penn, where the hell have you been?" he said hoarsely. "Do you realize what time it is? You shouldn't have been driving. You scared the hell out of me."

"Stephen is dead," Penn said abruptly.

"Dead!" gasped his father, going white. "What happened?"

"Motorcycle accident," I put in.

"You—you weren't charged, were you?" Penn's dad gaped at us. I realized Dr. Parrish was still focused on how Penn shouldn't have been driving while he was on pain medication. He seemed to have the idea that Penn had run Stephen down while in a drug-induced haze.

"I didn't hit him," said Penn. "He ran into a police car."

"You saw it?" asked Dr. Parrish.

"I drove up right afterward," said Penn. His hand was shaking, and he put it down on the table suddenly. "We just came from the scene of the accident."

"My God! Do his parents know?" asked Dr. Parrish, struggling to his feet.

"Sit down, Dad," said Penn in a flat voice. "Do you want to know the truth?" Penn gave me a long look, then turned back to his father. "Then you'd better sit down, because I'm going to tell you."

*　　*　　*

It was after four when we stopped talking. We had to go over some parts more than once. It was hard for Penn's father to take in so much dismaying news at once—Stephen a murderer. Penn acting as an accessory after the fact. Penn and I throwing the incriminating typewriter in the river, destroying evidence and lying to the police. I know we must have kept repeating ourselves. It seemed we were going around in circles like gerbils on an exercise wheel. Maybe it was because we were so tired.

When at last our story petered out, Penn's dad was pale. "We've got to get you a good lawyer," he said breathlessly.

Mugs of cocoa sat on the table, their bottoms full of chocolate dregs. The clock on the wall made a soft whirring noise in the silence.

"I don't think we need a lawyer," said Penn, glancing at me. "Stephen is dead. It's all over. What would be the point in telling all this stuff to the police? What good would it do anybody now for us to turn ourselves in for being accessories? We didn't really hurt anybody." Penn hesitated a moment. "Not on purpose, anyway."

Dr. Parrish closed his eyes. "I don't think the police would see it that way." He shook his head.

"Never in my wildest dreams . . ." he muttered. "And when I think that I recommended Joanna to Mrs. Landen! I'll never be able to look the woman in the face again."

I flushed hotly. I had felt uncomfortable about using Mrs. Landen, but that hadn't stopped me from doing it. I knew I deserved Dr. Parrish's reproach.

He got up. "I'd better call the hospital and check on her condition," he said. "If she dies, I won't be able to forgive myself."

Moving haltingly, he walked out of the room.

"Maybe I shouldn't have told him," Penn said bleakly.

I squeezed his hand.

When Penn's dad came back, he was dressed and looked more like his normal self. "Mrs. Landen told the ER doctor not to tell me, but she had been eating potato chips."

Penn grinned. I looked from one of them to the other. I didn't get it. What was the deal with potato chips?

"Salt is really bad for people with congestive heart disease," Penn explained.

"I warned her that if she went back to eating salt, she was going to end up in the hospital," said Dr. Parrish with grim satisfaction.

I sat there for a while, trying to make sense of

what they had said. "Is it possible she didn't hear a thing?" I asked wonderingly. "All that glass breaking, the screaming—"

"She probably thought it was the neighbors watching their television," said Penn.

"Joanna," said Dr. Parrish, "I've made up the bed in the spare room for you. There's no use your going home at this hour." He tugged impatiently at his shirt collar. "I'm going over to talk to Stephen's parents."

"Dad—" Penn began.

"I don't see any point in telling them everything," Dr. Parrish said, interrupting him. "It's bad enough that the boy is dead." He hesitated. "Casey's parents will have to be told, you realize. You can't let them go on thinking that he killed himself." He jingled his car keys in his pocket. "I only wish you had told me the truth to begin with." His voice was agonized.

Penn sighed. "I know, Dad. I know."

"You can come to me with anything. Anything," he said. "I thought you knew that."

The long silence was painful.

Dr. Parrish heaved a long sigh. "We're just going to have to do our best with this," he said. "It's bad. I don't know. . . ."

Penn's unhappy gaze met mine.

"Well, I'd better go," said Penn's dad. "We can talk about it when I get back." The door closed behind him with finality. Penn and I sat in silence, listening to his car start up in the garage. A minute later we saw his gray Continental gleam under the streetlight and then glide away.

Penn held his head in his hands. "It would have been nice," Penn said bitterly, "if he'd said he could understand how it could happen. Something like that."

He might as well ask for the dead to come back to life, I thought wearily. How could Dr. Parrish ever understand the complex web of love and fear and loyalty that had led us down such a terrible path? At times I could barely understand it myself.

"'You can come to me with anything,'" Penn mimicked his father's tone. "Right!"

"He's doing the best he can, Penn. It's just—anybody would find it tough to take. It's such a shock."

"I don't expect a gold medal. Just—'I can see how it was, Penn.' That's all I want him to say."

"But he probably can't see how it was," I suggested reasonably. Murder and blackmail probably didn't turn up very often on the agenda of the local medical society.

"You're right," snorted Penn. "Everything he's ever done has been strictly fill in the blank—one, two, three. Straight. Buttoned down. Nothing messy in his life. Must be nice!"

Penn wasn't making sense, I realized. He felt rotten, so he was letting off steam and trying to justify himself when he must know what he'd done was hard to justify.

"My dad is different from me," he said after a pause. "So what else is new." He smiled crookedly. "And now he wants us to tell everybody and his brother. Casey's parents! Jeez, we might as well turn ourselves in right now."

"Maybe we could skip some of the details when we talk to Casey's parents," I suggested. "We could tell them there was an argument and a struggle and the gun went off in Stephen's hand, and that then we were too scared to let on what happened. It's the truth, isn't it?"

"I don't know." Penn pressed his fingertips against his closed eyes. "I don't know what's true anymore. And I don't know what to do. I'm just so tired."

"Maybe the lawyers will tell us what we ought to do," I said.

"Lawyers!" snorted Penn. "Great! Yeah, well, having lawyers around is going to make everything just perfect." He glanced over at the stove. "You want some breakfast?" he asked.

I stifled a yawn. "Maybe so."

"Hey, what happened to your hand?" he said suddenly.

I looked at my bandage curiously, as if it belonged to somebody else. It hurt, but somehow I had forgotten about it. "When the door shattered, some glass ended up on the bed," I said. "I must have cut myself on it before I figured out what was going on."

"Is it okay?"

"Oh, sure."

"Maybe you ought to get some stitches in it."

I thought of a white-coated stranger sewing up my hand, and shuddered. "It's fine," I said.

Penn got up and measured coffee into a drip coffeemaker. "Are you sure you ought to drink that?" I asked. "With your headache?"

"I need caffeine, Joanna. Lay off me, will you? I've had just about all I can take."

"I'm going to take a bath," I said, my voice formal. "Will you please show me where the towels are?"

Without a word he led me out of the kitchen. Penn's house was vast. The large entry hall had a floor of handsome green-veined marble. From the hall graceful sweeping stairs rose to the top floor. My shoes sank deep into the carpeting as I climbed the stairs. The upstairs hallway was so long, it seemed to call for roller skates. I wondered if the house's air of heavy respectability was causing the chill that had suddenly fallen on us.

"Thank you," I said politely when Penn handed me an armful of thick towels from the linen closet.

"There's plenty of hot water," he said, struggling to produce a feeble smile. "It's not like it was out at the cabin."

He left me then and went downstairs. I stepped in the shower and let the hot water pummel me until my skin was numb. Then I dried off with thick bath towels the size of sheets. I felt sick to my stomach with the fear I was losing Penn. What if he hated the sight of me? I thought. I must remind him of the terrible times we'd been through. It would only be natural if he didn't want to be around me now. The past few months had been bad, but that would be the worst of all—losing Penn. What would I do without him?

When I got out, my legs were pink with steam and I was tingling all over and dizzy with fatigue. I pulled on my jeans and shirt and went downstairs.

The rain had begun again and was drizzling down the window, blurring the shrubs outside. The telephone pole on the street corner looked gray and crooked. The kitchen smelled of coffee. Penn popped some frozen waffles into the toaster. "I'm sorry," he said without turning around. "I bit your head off a minute ago, and I really am sorry. I don't know what's the matter with me. I'm not even making sense."

I put my arms loosely around his waist and let my head rest on his back.

He turned around and drew me close. His eyes were dark and blurred with tears. I felt a sharp sweet pang of love, so strong that it hurt. "We're going to be all right," I murmured softly. "The bad part's over. Now everything's going to be okay."

We held each other tight for a long time, our faces slick with tears, snuffling. I groped for a tissue and blew my nose.

The waffles popped up from the toaster. Penn pulled them out and laid them before me with several slices of butter and a bottle of syrup. "We've got to go tell Tessa, you know," he said.

"Penn!" I cried. "No!"

"Who's going to tell her, Joanna? She's not next of kin or anything."

I realized that was what Penn had been tensely waiting for. He had been waiting for morning so we could go tell Tessa.

"We can't let her hear it on the morning news," he said in a strained voice.

He was right, I realized. We had to go tell Tessa. But I shrank from it as flesh shrinks from a razor.

Before we left, I scrawled a note for Penn's dad so he would know where we had gone. Outside, the street was freckled with wet, fallen leaves and shiny with puddles. We drove in silence. I was sick and numb.

At Tessa's, the blinds were drawn and the only sign of life was the heat pump shuddering violently on the side of the house.

Penn knocked on the door and then rang the bell. It was several minutes before a plump woman with tousled dark hair came to the front door. She held her bathrobe closed with one hand. "Penn!" She blinked at him. I could hear the sound of Saturday-morning cartoons coming from the back of the house.

"Is Tessa up?" asked Penn. "I'm afraid we've got some bad news—about Stephen."

Her hand flew to cover her mouth. "Oh, no! The motorcycle! It's the motorcycle, isn't it? He's been in an accident. Is he in the hospital? Is he going to be all right?"

Penn shook his head. "He's dead."

Mrs. West's face crumpled and her eyes filled with tears.

"Mom!" I heard Tessa's voice. She was coming down the stairs. "Have you seen that envelope that came yesterday from Princeton?"

We stepped inside. Tessa stood on the stairs in jeans and a cotton sweater. The soles of her feet were bare and pink like a child's, and her hair was in tangled curls. She looked at us, her eyes suddenly watchful. "What are you two doing here?" she asked.

"Tessie, come on down," wheedled her mother.

Slowly Tessa walked down. I had never realized before how graceful she was and how heartbreakingly beautiful. All at once I saw why Stephen couldn't bear to lose her.

"Mom, you don't have to hang around anymore," said Tessa. "I can talk to them by myself."

Penn and I exchanged a glance. Tessa thought we had come to tell her some bad news about evidence uncovered or witnesses. She was still worried about the police.

Mrs. West took a wadded tissue out of the pocket of her bathrobe and dabbed at her eyes.

Penn opened his mouth and looked at me helplessly. He couldn't seem to speak.

"Stephen's been in a motorcycle accident," I said finally. "He's dead."

"No!" Tessa shrieked, her voice high and inhuman like a bird's. "No! It's not true!"

"I saw it, Tess," said Penn. "Or almost did. He ran into a police car and was thrown off the bike. It happened so fast, I don't think he knew what happened."

"That's a lie!" Tessa whimpered, pressing her fist to her mouth. "He always wore his helmet. He promised me he would! He promised me." She wheeled around to face her mother. "You can go now, Mom."

Her mother patted her on the shoulder. "No, dear. I'll stay right here with you."

"No!" shrieked Tessa. "Go away. Leave me alone!"

Her mother shot us a meaningful look. "I'll be right in the kitchen if you need me."

Tessa watched her mother's retreating back and, when she was gone, grabbed Penn by the shoulders and stared into his eyes. "Tell me the truth, Penn. Did you do it?" I scarcely recognized her voice. It was harsh and thin.

Penn was visibly shaken. "I promise you, Tess, I didn't lay a hand on him. I couldn't. You know I couldn't."

"Then how could it happen?" She wiped her nose with her palm. Her face was slick and slobbery with tears. "It wasn't supposed to happen," she sobbed. "He was just eighteen."

Penn's agonized glance met mine. "He was running away, Tess. I don't think he had time to put on his helmet. He broke into Mrs. Landen's house, but he wasn't expecting Joanna to be there. When he saw her, he panicked and took off."

"No!" whispered Tessa. "You've got it mixed up."

"It's true," I said. "He threw a cement block through the sliding glass door. There was glass all over the shoes of his soles."

"Stop! Shut up! I've got to go to him," cried Tessa.

Her mother came running back and put her arm around her. "My poor baby! I'm going to call Dr. Proctor and get you a nice sedative so you can sleep."

"Don't try to stop me, Mama," Tessa said desperately. "I'm going to go to him."

I saw wild panic in Mrs. West's eyes. "Lawrence!" she cried.

Tessa's dad came running in. Scraps of white shaving lather still clung to his jowls, and though he was dressed, he didn't have shoes on, and he slipped a little on the tile floor of the foyer. "Talk to her," cried Mrs. West.

Tessa threw her head on her father's chest and sobbed. I couldn't understand most of what she was saying. He patted her back. "There, there, baby. It's bad. I know it's bad. You just go ahead and cry. Daddy's here." He glanced at Penn and said in quite a different voice, "Penn, where've they taken him?"

"My dad would know. He's probably back at home by now."

"We'd better go now," I said, tugging at Penn's hand. "Let's go."

Tessa's mother hugged us both, weeping. But at last we escaped her and stepped out into the cool morning air. "Do you think they're going to drive over to the morgue?" I asked, gazing at the gray drizzle around us. Rain was dripping down my collar and beading in a fine veil on my hair, but it didn't seem to matter.

"Probably," Penn said shortly. He hunched his shoulders as if he were protecting himself from a blow from behind.

. . . *Did Tessa have to know the truth about Stephen? I keep asking myself miserably. Were we wrong to tell her about the burglary and about the broken glass on his shoes? Newspaper reporters pick up these stories off of police reports. The burglary is going to show up in the newspaper, I tell myself. She had to know.*

Maybe it doesn't really make any difference what I told her anyway. All that matters now is that Stephen is dead.

Twenty

Dear Diary,

As I write, fatigue burns my eyes and makes me woozy. The walls of the foyer at Penn's house seem to swell and recede, and the prisms in the chandelier over the staircase shoot confusing splinters of light over the green marble. I think of the cabin in the woods, gone up now in smoke, and of the endless card games we played there, the smell of bread baking, the sound of the rain drumming on the roof and streaming down the big plate-glass windows.

"I think we'd better get some sleep." Penn yawned.

We seemed to be moving in slow motion as

we climbed the stairs. Outside the guest room, Penn put his fingers under my chin, tilted my face up, and kissed me lingeringly. I clung to him as if I were afraid he would vanish. So much that I had loved had vanished.

"I don't think I've ever been so tired in my life," he said in a flat-sounding voice.

My arms fell to my side and we drew away from each other.

In our separate bedrooms we slept the sleep of the dead. If I dreamed, I have no memory of it. I seemed to black out.

When at last I came to, sun was shining through the leaves of the oak outside my window, and they were glittery with rain. The thin sunshine coming in the window cast a jagged pattern on the carpet. My mouth was cottony and my clothes felt damp and warmly sticky. What I wanted above all was clean, dry clothes. When I stepped out into the hall, I could hear a shower was running somewhere.

I went downstairs and found Penn's dad in the kitchen fixing sandwiches. The kitchen smelled strongly of tuna fish. I remembered Penn saying that theirs was a household that always stocked tuna fish, tofu, and soybean burgers. No wonder Penn never put on any weight. Dr.

Parrish smiled. "Thanks for leaving me the note," he said. "How is Tessa?"

"About the way you'd expect. She's absolutely crazy and would throw herself into his grave if she could."

"Terrible." He shook his head. "Terrible." There was a long silence, and then he said in quite a different voice, "Would you like a tuna fish sandwich?"

I hate tuna fish sandwiches. "I think I'll have dry toast and milk," I said.

Through the window I watched the mail carrier going along the sidewalk, a bag slung over his shoulder and a terrier yipping at his heels. Somewhere a car door slammed.

Penn came thundering down the stairs and bounced into the kitchen. The wheat-colored fisherman's sweater he had on was pushed up on the arms and sagged a bit below his collarbone. His hair, still wet, was the color of honey and showed the marks of a comb pulled through it. I wanted desperately to kiss him.

"Somebody named Bobby Jenkins called," said Dr. Parrish. "Is he some relative of Laurie's?"

Before Penn could answer, the phone rang. I wished I could wave a magic wand and we would magically be on a tropical island, lying on the warm sand and smothering each other with kisses. I loved him so much it hurt. Outside the window, cold rain dripped. I could hear the hiss of the wheels of a passing car.

"Hi," Penn said into the phone. There was a long silence. "Sure," he said. "I guess we could do that. Okay." He hung up and glanced at me. "Bobby wants us to meet him for lunch at the Rathskeller."

"What?" protested Dr. Parrish with false heartiness. "And miss out on my tuna fish sandwiches?"

"Sorry to disappoint you, Dad, but we don't want to get on Bobby's wrong side." Penn smiled crookedly. "Do we, Joanna?"

"Nobody wants to get on Bobby's wrong side," I agreed. "He's big."

Dr. Parrish put a couple of slices of whole-wheat bread in the toaster. "Well," he cleared his throat, "I've talked to some people already, and I've lined it up for you to go talk to a very good lawyer on Monday."

Penn shrugged.

"Joanna will want to get her own representation, of course," Dr. Parrish went on. "Her father can take care of that."

My heart sank. I dreaded talking to my father. I wanted to cry out to Dr. Parrish, "Let me stay here! Adopt me! I don't ever want to go home!"

Penn drove me back to Mrs. Landen's house so I could let myself in, change clothes, and retrieve my car. The bedroom was dark now since the police had nailed plywood over the broken sliding glass door.

Penn's astonished eyes took in the silver-dollar-sized splashes of blood on the bed and carpet, the long shards of broken glass on the carpet, and the cement block sitting incongruously in front of the maple dressing table.

"Good God," he said faintly.

"How much are we going to tell Bobby?" I asked him.

"I don't know." He shook his head.

"Then I'll let you do the talking," I said.

"Hasn't it hit you that Bobby has some explaining of his own to do?" asked Penn. "What was he doing charging into your bedroom last night?"

Bobby was to meet us at the Rathskeller, but it was so dark inside, I wondered how we would find him without a flashlight. The Rathskeller, which was on the campus of the local college, featured an array of vegetarian dishes and burgers served in dark rooms with wooden booths.

Penn glanced at me. "Do you have the feeling we're going to meet an animal in his lair?"

I punched him. "Cut it out, Penn."

He raised a hand, fending me off. "Don't say it. I know what you're going to say." He mimicked me: "'Bobby's not so bad, Penn.'"

I spoke to a passing waitress. "We're meeting a friend," I said. "A big fellow?"

She led us at once to Bobby, who was glowering over a burger in a corner booth of the back room. A foaming mug of beer was at his elbow.

"How did you get a beer?" I asked, surprised.

"I ordered one," he said.

They were probably afraid to say no, I thought.

I decided it was best to take the offensive. "Bobby, what were you doing at Mrs. Landen's?" I asked sternly. "I nearly fainted when I heard your voice."

"I was watching the house," said Bobby. "You were acting so weird, I knew something had to be up. And then, when I came just before dark to finish the hedge, I spotted Stephen. He was on that motorcycle of his up at the corner, watching me. I thought, What the heck is going on here? So I hung around to find out."

"You hung around until one A.M.?" I asked him incredulously.

"I parked up the street a ways. There's a house there with some newspapers piled up, so I figured they're on vacation and I sat in their driveway. All of a sudden I heard a motorcycle and I woke up. But I didn't see a motorcycle. All I saw was this guy in black leather from head to foot walking up to Mrs. Landen's house. Next thing I knew, he was going around back and I saw he was carrying something heavy. I knew something was wrong. So I shook myself awake and jumped out of the car to go after him. It was wet, and the grass was so slippery I ended up falling flat on my face. Next thing I knew, I heard this big crash and somebody's screaming. I got up, ran around back, then up on the deck and I see the glass door's gone. I go right after the guy, glass falling all over the place—I was lucky I didn't get slashed. Stupidest way to break into a house I ever saw."

"I think he wanted to make a lot of noise," put in Penn.

"He was trying to scare Mrs. Landen to death," I suggested.

"Yeah," said Penn. "I don't think he wanted to shoot her."

"Nice guy," said Bobby sarcastically.

"You ran right into him," I told Bobby. "I couldn't figure out what was going on at first. I was so sure it was Stephen, but then I heard your voice."

"Well, first," said Bobby, "I ran into something in the middle of the floor. I got this ringing pain right up to my hip and I'm seeing stars."

"You must have hit the cement block," I said.

"It hurt like hell," groused Bobby. "And before I've even quit seeing stars, the guy runs right into me."

"That was Stephen," I said.

"Yeah. So then you know what happened. I ran after him, but he was ahead of me and I lost him. Next thing I know this bike comes roaring out and I go after him."

"That's probably why he wrecked the bike," I said. "He was so rattled. You were right on his heels, and he must have heard the sirens, too."

Bobby frowned. "What was he after? Why was he breaking into Mrs. Landen's house in the first place? What did he have against her? I know she's an old biddy, but it wasn't like he had to put up with her."

Taking a deep breath, I explained to Bobby about the grade and how Mrs. Landen had found out it had been changed, and had lodged a complaint.

"You mean all this was because of a stupid grade!" exclaimed Bobby.

"Well, a lot depended on it. He was hoping to get into Princeton, for one thing, and when that didn't work out, he still had the National Merit Scholarship."

"Who cares about a stupid grade?" said Bobby scornfully.

Not Bobby, obviously.

"He must have been out of his mind," Bobby concluded.

I shivered. "Lucky for me he didn't shoot me. Here I was screaming and heaving things at him, showing him right where I was."

"Yeah, but he didn't expect you to be there," Penn pointed out. "It must have really thrown him. I bet he didn't even have a gun with him. He didn't need one to kill an old lady like Mrs. Landen. He probably thought she'd keel over when she heard all that glass break. An old lady, alone at night and with a serious heart condition. He figured he wouldn't have to lay a hand on her."

"His favorite kind of murder," I said. "Where everything looks natural."

"What do you mean by that?" asked Bobby, glancing at us. "Are you trying to tell me he was the one who killed Laurie?"

My eyes met Penn's. I wasn't sure how to field this one. I didn't like to admit to Bobby that we had known all along what had happened.

"I guess we'll never know for sure," said Penn. "But I have my suspicions. I've—" He cleared his throat. "I've always wondered if Laurie didn't fall off that cliff up on Lookout Point. You know her body was found not that far from there. Stephen could have gotten mad at her and pushed her over and then tried to hide what happened."

"The bastard." Bobby's face was dark. "I wonder if she found out about his grade, and that's why he killed her."

"Maybe," said Penn.

Bobby peered at us closely through the gloom. "Funny thing—I figured whatever it was, you were all in it together. You looked awfully tight to me."

"We used to be," said Penn in an odd voice. He squeezed my hand painfully hard. "But it seems like a long time ago," he said.

*   *   *

As Penn was driving me home, I said, "We lied to Bobby."

"Okay, we lied a little bit," Penn admitted. "Here and there."

A long silence fell. I felt wobbly and out of control. What did I want? Everything tied up neatly in a package with blue ribbons? Or did I want something that I couldn't have—like a clear conscience?

"Okay, we aren't perfect," Penn went on. "But this is sort of a compromise I can live with."

"You're right." I stiffened my shoulders. "After all, a few days ago, it looked as if there was no way out for us."

I could hear the whisper of the steering wheel brushing against Penn's palms as he turned. "This is our second chance," he said. He smiled at me a little sadly. "The way I figure it—we get to start over."

I smiled. "You're right. It's a second chance. I think we'd better take it." I glanced at the speedometer. "Slow down, Penn."

A broad smile spread across his face.

. . . What an odd feeling it is to be free! The wind blows through my hair, tugging at

it, whipping it into my mouth and making me laugh. Silly, stupid things can make me laugh now. It's not that I'm happy exactly— but that I'm relieved. I breathe so deep that it makes me cough, and then I laugh at myself for being glad to be alive.

Epilogue

State University was as full of people as a city, yet I never seemed to run into anyone that I knew—except for Penn. Nikki Warren was going to State, but I never saw her once. Sometimes I thought of Mrs. Landen's advice about not running around too much with my old friends from high school, and I smiled a little ruefully.

I think about what happened quite a lot, actually. I think about the first time Penn sent me roses, their red beauty blazing. And the fuzzy caterpillars that fell from the trees at the cabin in spring. A lot of them are turned to butterflies by now, I suppose. I think about Casey in his coffin, Laurie's body turning soft and rotting under a pile of leaves, and of Stephen, his loose dark locks matted with blood.

Penn and I came home at fall midterm break. We hadn't planned on it, but so many people cleared out as soon as midterms were over that the campus was like a ghost town. Maybe we felt the deathlike tinge of the place more than most people would. It was depressing, so we packed up and left.

Midterm break happened to be the weekend of the Down East Festival in Barton City. The main street of town had been roped off and was filled with vendors selling lemonade, cotton candy, carved paper-towel covers, doll beds, and rocking chairs. Square dancers were dancing on a raised platform, bands were playing in the parking lots of banks, and over by the city hall, participants in the barbecue contest were basting roast pigs.

Penn and I walked arm in arm, making our way past groups of giggling teens and young families with sticky-faced toddlers. The sun was beating hot on our heads. We spotted Captain Kronkie walking blond twins who looked to be about five.

"It's Kronkie," said Penn. "Do we speak to him or run away?"

What Penn's father referred to as our "legal problems" had receded to the edge of our consciousness lately. We had decided to offer only minimal explanations to the police. It was obvious Stephen had broken into Mrs. Landen's house, and we volunteered, in all confidence, to the police, that we had been concerned about him lately and had wondered whether he might not have had something to do with Laurie's death. I don't know how much of it they believed, but to our relief they appeared to have bigger fish to fry than us. Despite our worst fears, our likenesses had not yet appeared on *America's Most Wanted*.

"Hello," said Captain Kronkie, surveying us with his cool eyes. "How's school?"

"Fine," said Penn.

"Fine," I echoed.

"It's been awfully quiet out at the high school since you kids graduated," he said.

"What does he mean by that?" Penn asked resentfully after we had passed them.

"You know what it means, Penn—it means he doesn't like us, doesn't trust us, and doesn't believe us, but it doesn't matter anymore. Forget it!"

Suddenly I spotted Tessa. She was perched on a bar stool at the Tasty Freeze concession, her thin skirt riding halfway up one shapely leg. I mistook her for someone down from New York at first and almost didn't recognize her. When I did, my heart gave a queer squeeze. She saw us coming and flung out her arms.

Penn ran over to her and hugged her so tightly, she was lifted off the bar stool. "How's Princeton?" he asked.

She laughed. "Great! Absolutely fantastic!" she said. "It's beautiful, and I've met the most fabulous people. You'll have to come up there and see me sometime. I'd love for you to meet my friends."

"Sure. We'll have to do that," said Penn.

We all knew we never would.

"Well, you guys." She looked at us both. "How's State?"

"Good," I said.

"We got an apartment off campus so we don't have to eat cafeteria food," said Penn.

"Penn's learning to cook," I said.

"Neat!" cried Tessa. "It's just so good to see you guys!" She rummaged in her tiny bag, pulled out a pack of cigarettes, and tapped one out of the pack. She struck a match, touched it to the cigarette, and inhaled deeply.

"I didn't know you smoked," I said.

Her eyes were confused for a minute. "I don't, really. Well, not much, anyway." She held the cigarette between two fingers and with a slightly puzzled look watched the smoke curl away from it. "I don't know," she said. "I like the smell. It—it comforts me." I saw then that her eyes were shiny with tears.

"How's the frozen yogurt?" I asked hastily.

She dabbed at her eyes with a tissue. "Okay. It's good, really. At Princeton we have the best food." She smiled. "My roommate is the world's worst slob. Every shirt she owns has a footprint square in the middle of the back. Have you ever heard of laying all your clothes out on the floor?"

"Lots of people do it," Penn assured her.

We sat down on the bar stools and ordered yogurt. The seats were hot and the sun beat on our backs. The frozen yogurt melted and turned to foam almost before we got our spoons in, and I had to crane my neck around Penn to see Tessa. I flexed my hand self-consciously, looking at the long white scar that ran along the base of my thumb. I guessed I should have gotten some stitches in it. The three of us talked awkwardly about the classes we were taking. Chemistry and differential equations were hard. Physics was easy because Dockerty had been so tough, everything was smooth sailing after that. Before long we ran out of things to say. I think it was because there was so much we couldn't say.

When we got up to leave, Tessa grabbed our hands and held on tightly. Her eyes were brimming, and she seemed to be trying to memorize our faces. The cigarette smoked unheeded in a plastic ashtray as if it belonged to a ghost. Maybe it did.

"It's so great to see you guys," she said. "We ought to try to get together sometime and really talk."

"Sure," said Penn. "We'll give you a call over Christmas."

She squeezed our hands. "No hard feelings, okay?"

Penn bent over and kissed her cheek.

Dear Diary,

I think about Tessa sometimes, but I hear she isn't coming home for Christmas after all. She's taken up with a bodybuilder and they're going skiing in the Alps over the holidays. Can this be true? Penn says anything is possible.

Some few things we saved from the ruins: herb tea, the smell of good bread, the memories—and our lives. I suppose we are haunted by our memories. Moonlit nights are hard. Penn draws me close in his arms in the hope that his presence will drive away the bad dreams. Sometimes it works. When we go out to eat, we always choose the no-smoking section.

About the Author

Janice Harrell lives in North Carolina. She has written numerous books for young adults and adults.

THRILLERS

R.L. Stine

- ☐ MC44236-8 The Baby-sitter $3.50
- ☐ MC44332-1 The Baby-sitter II $3.50
- ☐ MC46099-4 The Baby-sitter III $3.50
- ☐ MC45386-6 Beach House $3.25
- ☐ MC43278-8 Beach Party $3.50
- ☐ MC43125-0 Blind Date $3.50
- ☐ MC43279-6 The Boyfriend $3.50
- ☐ MC44333-X The Girlfriend $3.50
- ☐ MC45385-8 Hit and Run $3.25
- ☐ MC46100-1 The Hitchhiker $3.50
- ☐ MC43280-X The Snowman $3.50
- ☐ MC43139-0 Twisted $3.50

Caroline B. Cooney

- ☐ MC44316-X The Cheerleader $3.25
- ☐ MC41641-3 The Fire $3.25
- ☐ MC43806-9 The Fog $3.25
- ☐ MC45681-4 Freeze Tag $3.25
- ☐ MC45402-1 The Perfume $3.25
- ☐ MC44884-6 The Return of the Vampire $2.95
- ☐ MC41640-5 The Snow $3.25
- ☐ MC45682-2 The Vampire's Promise $3.50

Diane Hoh

- ☐ MC44330-5 The Accident $3.25
- ☐ MC45401-3 The Fever $3.25
- ☐ MC43050-5 Funhouse $3.25
- ☐ MC44904-4 The Invitation $3.50
- ☐ MC45640-7 The Train $3.25

Sinclair Smith

- ☐ MC45063-8 The Waitress $2.95

Christopher Pike

- ☐ MC43014-9 Slumber Party $3.50
- ☐ MC44256-2 Weekend $3.50

A. Bates

- ☐ MC45829-9 The Dead Game $3.25
- ☐ MC43291-5 Final Exam $3.25
- ☐ MC44582-0 Mother's Helper $3.50
- ☐ MC44238-4 Party Line $3.25

D.E. Athkins

- ☐ MC45246-0 Mirror, Mirror $3.25
- ☐ MC45349-1 The Ripper $3.25
- ☐ MC44941-9 Sister Dearest $2.95

Carol Ellis

- ☐ MC46411-6 Camp Fear $3.25
- ☐ MC44768-8 My Secret Admirer $3.25
- ☐ MC46044-7 The Stepdaughter $3.25
- ☐ MC44916-8 The Window $2.95

Richie Tankersley Cusick

- ☐ MC43115-3 April Fools $3.25
- ☐ MC43203-6 The Lifeguard $3.25
- ☐ MC43114-5 Teacher's Pet $3.25
- ☐ MC44235-X Trick or Treat $3.25

Lael Littke

- ☐ MC44237-6 Prom Dress $3.25

Edited by T. Pines

- ☐ MC45256-8 Thirteen $3.50

Available wherever you buy books, or use this order form.